A
Harlequin
Romance

OTHER
Harlequin Romances
by DOROTHY CORK

Many of these titles are available at your local bookseller,
or through the Harlequin Reader Service.

For a free catalogue listing all available Harlequin Romances,
send your name and address to:

HARLEQUIN READER SERVICE,
M.P.O. Box 707, Niagara Falls, N.Y. 14302
Canadian address: Stratford, Ontario, Canada N5A 6W4

or use coupon at back of book.

WANDALILLI PRINCESS

by

DOROTHY CORK

HARLEQUIN BOOKS   TORONTO
WINNIPEG

Harlequin edition published November 1975

SBN 373-01927-0

Original hard cover edition published in 1975
by Mills & Boon Limited.

All the characters in this book have no existence outside the
imagination of the Author, and have no relation whatsoever to
anyone bearing the same name or names. They are not even
distantly inspired by any individual known or unknown to the
Author, and all the incidents are pure invention.

CHAPTER ONE

FRAZER pulled up at the wide, white-barred gate that bore the name Wandalilli in black lettering, and waited for an instant before she climbed out of the car to open it. The mail box at one side was designated Dexter – meticulous, unmistakable – and she looked at it unblinkingly, her violet-blue eyes, darkly framed by smudged in lashes, carefully expressionless. Dexter was a name she had hated for four years. Dexter was a man she had never met, but whom she had deliberately planned to meet today.

Crazy? Maybe. But it had to be, because this was the place to come to look for opals.

It had been Frazer's dream – no, that was too soft and flimsy a way of putting it— It had been Frazer's *fiery ambition*, her one and only desire, to mine for opals, to continue her father's dream, as soon as her schooldays were done, and she had finished with school two months ago. The fever – the opal fever – was in her blood as it had been in her father's. It was something that couldn't be denied unless you were physically weak or lacking in character, and Frazer was neither of those things.

Summer would soon be on the way out, but now the sun was still burningly hot out here on the tree scattered plain where the long ridges rolled down, low and endless, strangely beautiful to Frazer with their spiked silvery grasses, their stands of stunted acacias. Those ridges were desert sandstone and underneath was opal dirt. The thought excited her. She wished she could get to work right away, and she touched momentarily the tiny diamond-shaped opal that hung from a gold chain, hidden inside her black cotton shirt. For a second she wondered if it had been a mistake to wear her favourite black jeans and shirt instead of one of the cool pretty dresses that turned her into the Cathleen Frazer Madigan of whom Aunt Helen approved. Well, she wasn't here to impress anyone – particularly not Dexter or the Old Man ...

In the pocket of her jeans she had a reporter's notebook and a pencil, though she wasn't sure whether or not she was going to use them. She wasn't really a newspaper reporter, it was pretence in a way, because it wasn't what she wanted to do. She was playing at it – writing the odd social paragraph, interviewing a few outback housewives – to please Uncle Frank who ran the *Mingari Star*. Just till summer was ended and the sun had lost its fierce heat and she could peg out a claim and look for opal.

She pushed back her gold-streaked light brown hair, climbed out of the car and opened the gate, and a minute later had driven through, shut the gate, and was heading for the homestead. It didn't look too bad, the countryside, she thought, eyeing it critically. She could see a scattering of cattle on the flat plain she was travelling across – feeding on the drying grasses, resting in the scrub or under the belahs and wilgas and coolibahs. One or two of them looked at the car impassively as she drove by and she said ironically, 'How do you do? I'm going to see your master.' It would have been much easier not to have had to bother about Dexter, simply to have turned up on her motorbike in a couple of weeks' time, pitched her tent, and got to work. But that was not possible. She had to find a certain place, and she didn't know where it was except it was on the Wandalilli cattle run – and that covered an area of heaven knew how many thousand acres. An old shaft, put down by her father over four years ago; the mine where he had been so confident he would find precious opal – and the gem of his dreams – the one that would be named, as all the finest opals are given a name. The Añdamooka Queen, the Star of Bethlehem, the Red Admiral – Lee Madigan's opal was going to be not a Queen but a Princess – for Frazer. He had always called her Princess when they were alone, though she was Frazer on the fields.

But he had never found his Princess, his heart's desire, because he had not lived long enough. He had been taken

6

to hospital too late for an operation and had died with a ruptured appendix – all because the Dexters, who resented his mining on their precious land, had found it too much trouble to help him when he asked. He had told Frazer what sort of people they were the last time she ever saw him, when he paid her a visit at the boarding school in Sydney, so she knew.

The station homestead came into sight as she swung the car round a curve at the foot of a ridge. It stood on a slope in a grove of trees. She could see the long low red roof of the house, and away from it other buildings – garages, the men's quarters, the work-shed probably. Frazer had visited a few cattle and sheep stations in the past few weeks in the course of her work. Till then, she had never been on an outback property, though her mother, who had died when she was six years old, had been brought up on a cattle station further east. Frazer had never met her maternal grandparents. They were dead now, but they had never been interested in her. In fact, they had put Frazer's mother Frances completely out of their lives when she married Liam Madigan. 'Big-headed, high-handed snobs,' Lee had called them. 'I never wanted their money, but it would have helped to have had a bit for Francie when she was ill.'

Frazer pulled up near the gate that led into the homestead garden. The drive curved round past the garages, and she saw a car in there and a couple of motorbikes which she supposed were used for working the property. She left the car and went through the garden feeling her heart begin to beat just a little bit faster. As she tapped on the wire screen door, she saw there was a woman sitting on the verandah reading. Slim, thirtyish, dark-haired, conventional-looking – the sort of woman of whom Aunt Helen would approve. She came to the door and looked at Frazer through the fly screen – at her unpainted face, her black jeans and boots, her shirt with the sleeves pushed up.

'Yes?' Her voice was just on the cool side of neutral.

Frazer thought, 'She must be Dexter's wife.' She hadn't

7

planned on seeing his wife – or his father, the Old Man, either, really. She had taken it for granted she would see *him*, and she was going to say, 'There's an old opal mine on your land, Mr. Dexter. I want to know exactly where it is because I'm going to work it.' Just like that. She had written her lines mentally ages ago, while she was still at school. Head up, looking him straight in the eye – knowing what she knew about him but saying nothing. Yet.

Now, she found herself stammering a little as she asked, 'Is – is Mr. Dexter here?'

'No, he's not. He's over at the branding yards. What is it you want? We don't' – with a flick of her dark eyes over Frazer's clothes – 'we don't employ girls on Wandalilli.'

Frazer put her chin up. 'I don't want to be employed here. I'm looking for an old opal mine that's on your property.'

The other woman frowned faintly. 'I'm afraid you've made a mistake. There's no opal mine on this station, Miss–'

Frazer hesitated fractionally and then said, 'Dwight.' It was her uncle's name. She added just a little aggressively, 'I'm from the *Mingari Star* and – and I know there *is* a mine.'

'Then you've been misinformed, Miss Dwight. Quite definitely there is not a mine. If your paper sent you here, then you're on a wild goose chase. You won't find a mine and you won't find a story.'

Frazer's violet eyes met hers steadily. This woman was very plainly one of Them. 'I already have a story,' she said silently. 'A story you – or your husband – somehow managed to keep out of the papers years ago. A story about the kind of people who wouldn't help a man if he was dying – people called Dexter.' She wondered what this woman would say if she told her she was going to *work* that non-existent mine ... She said aloud, 'I think I'll find both. Where is the old shaft?'

It wasn't a manner that got results, of course, and now there was definite hostility in the other woman's dark eyes. She was told with a chilly civility, 'I'm sorry – I

8

can't help you. You're wasting your time. Good afternoon.'

Frazer faced her for a second, fuming inwardly. What did she do now? She *had* to find out where that shaft was – all her plans, all her ambitions, hinged on it. 'My whole future,' thought Frazer, because that was how it seemed. It was the only future she had ever envisaged. She turned slowly, and as she went down the steps she could see a cloud of red dust out across the plain and her heart lightened. Beasts, horses, men – the branding camp! Right – she would find Dexter.

It looked pretty bumpy going for Aunt Helen's car, and she had a sudden inspiration. Those motorbikes in the garage – she could nip over there on one of them in a flash! Now she was glad she had worn her jeans, had slipped away before Aunt Helen had caught her out. Because she had been supposedly driving to a sheep station to talk to one of the girls there about her wedding plans.

Frazer glanced back at the house. The woman had gone back to her book. She drove the car over to the garages, parked it in the shade of some tall eucalypts, chose one of the two motorbikes. She had ridden on the back of a motorbike since she was six years old, learned to ride one as soon as she was big enough. She loved motorbikes as some girls love horses – or cars. In a few seconds she was spinning down the track in the general direction of the branding yard. She couldn't see them now, because they were beyond the spur of the next ridge. Her gold-streaked hair flew back from her face and she felt free and happy and purposeful. The sun was hot – but this was the way to travel! – and she loved the feel of it on skin already golden from an outdoor life.

She reached the yards, and several heads turned. Male heads, every one of them, of course. Frazer dismounted and parked the bike under a tree, pushed the sleeves of her shirt a little higher – it was hot! – and walked into the swirling dust, conscious of the smell of burning hides, the haze of smoke, the tossing of heads and rolling of eyes amongst a mob of what looked to be mainly young beasts.

She looked over the men quickly as she moved. There had been a slight lull in operations and then the work continued – a rope was flung, a calf pulled down. The branding iron glowed, there was a scurry and more dust—

They were all tough-looking men, all dusty, all wearing narrow-legged trousers and wide-brimmed hats pulled down over their eyes. Frazer had been brought up used to the sight of tough, dusty-looking men – though in a rather different setting – so that didn't worry her a bit now. She wasn't exactly conscious of making a choice, but she swerved suddenly and made for a lean, dark, aggressive-looking type who stood against the rails, something masterful in the lazy grace of his relaxed posture.

He watched her come, and then he straightened up and smiled. Not exactly in a friendly way, but as if it was the thing to do. He had a wide mouth and white teeth, and the eyes that looked at her directly from under the shadow of a broad-brimmed hat were of so dark a brown that they were almost black. His hair was black too, where it showed under his hat. Frazer thought, 'He's as hard as the ironstone pebbles lying on the ground. And all these beasts and all this land are his, and these men are working for *him*. He's the Lord of the Winds, the King of the Plains, and doesn't he know it!' She was as certain as that that he was Dexter, and she was right – even though he was younger than she had expected, no more than thirty-three or four.

'Chin up,' she reminded herself subconsciously. 'Princess!' – and she smiled back at him, full of charm and full of assurance. Oh, she could do it all right – it was the way Aunt Helen liked her to smile at people – particularly eligible males – when she met them. 'Don't look as if you're ready to spring away, like some wild thing. You have a pretty mouth and pretty teeth, a smile can do wonders for you.'

'Well, hello,' he said, from four feet away. And close as this, she could see how dark and straight his lashes were, how lean and richly tanned his cheeks. 'I'm Jay Dexter. What can I do for you?' He looked at her gear, and then he looked at her smiling mouth, and her gold-flecked hair, his black eyes narrowed against the dust and the sunlight. His wide mouth curved a little crookedly, and somehow she knew that *he* was far from dazzled by her smile. That he was not, in fact, impressed. And while she worried about it fractionally, and reminded herself it was to be expected from *him*, he added, 'Shall I make a hopeful guess? You're a geology fanatic working on a school project. Your get-up's a bit aggressive, but I think I detect signs of untried years—'

Frazer's cheeks flamed. Untried years! She said chillingly and a little to her own surprise, 'I'm a reporter from the *Mingari Star* and I'm doing a story on opal mining.'

One eyebrow went up. 'Is that so? Well, this is a branding camp. There's no opal mining going on here, Miss—'

'Dwight,' she said, as automatically as though it were the truth. 'Cathleen Dwight. And I know this is a branding camp. I'm not an idiot.'

He ignored that. But he repeated, 'Dwight—' and screwed up one eye. 'Family job,' he commented. 'You're not a seasoned reporter. Isn't it Frank Dwight who runs the *Mingari Star*?'

'Yes, he's my uncle,' said Frazer, crimson-cheeked and hating him for so methodically cutting her down to size. Wishing even that she had stuck to her original plan, and simply demanded—

'Well, Kate,' he said, 'I repeat there's no opal mining going on here, so you go home and tell your uncle I said so. If you're looking for excitement, get him to send you out to Lightning Ridge or White Cliffs – though I'd suggest not on your own. You'll have no trouble getting some kind of a story there.'

Quizzical, patronizing, but impassive too, his eyes as hard and blank and discouraging as they could be.

Frazer bit her lip. She concentrated hard on remembering her father – the last time she had seen him – the last letter she had had from him. And this was the man who hadn't lifted a finger to help *him* . . . She dropped completely her somewhat shaky social façade and said bluntly, abruptly, 'There's a story here. Didn't a man' – she swallowed and with an effort kept her gaze steadily, accusingly on him– 'Didn't a man die here looking for opals? Wasn't there – a tragedy—'

His eyes grew even blacker. 'So you're looking for a sensation, are you? I don't know who put you or Frank Dwight on to this, but you've drawn a blank, Kate. No tragedy, no melodrama, no death on the site. A shaft was sunk – but nothing was found. Since then we've had the odd fossicker, but no one's ever found a thing. I just don't encourage so-called miners to come camping on my land. If they want opals, there are plenty of recognized fields where they can go to look for them. I've had enough of undesirable types flaunting their miner's rights.'

Frazer listened, bristling with hostility. Undesirable types! Did he count her father amongst those? No one could have said more clearly, 'Clear out – don't come here trying to dig up past history. Keep off *my* land.' What would he say if he knew that she would be camped on his land in a couple of weeks' time – she and Caryl and Robert Hill – gouging for the opals that she knew were there in the old shaft her own father had sunk? That was a surprise in store for him. And one day she would have pleasure in telling him all she knew – in reminding him—

'You're certainly not very helpful, are you?' she said coldly. Of course she wasn't looking for a story, and maybe she should have plunged right in and demanded, 'Just show me where the old shaft is.' But she had an idea he'd refuse point blank. And then what would she do? Her glance went quickly to the men in the branding yards, all of them very much occupied. Would any of them know?

He interpreted her glance and said unexpectedly, 'I'll show you the old shaft. Then you can run along home and tell your uncle you did your best. And by the way,' he added, with a glance at the bike, 'who told you you could make use of my property?'

'No one,' said Frazer. After all, a motorbike uses an infinitesimal amount of fuel, so there was nothing to make a fuss of. She hadn't stolen it. In any case, she couldn't be worried now, because he was going to show her her father's old mine. Inside she was all excitement mixed with a deep sadness, a kind of apprehension. Wondering if after all she could bear to see the very last place her father had ever worked the ground in his lifelong search for its treasure. But knowing at the same time that it was for him she was doing it – for him, and because she was like he had been, she too had opal fever on the brain ...

She was astride the bike and had started it up without paying any more attention to Dexter and his irrelevant complaints – looking round expectantly for a lead. He stood where he was, brows down, and she felt impatience – surely he wasn't going to quibble about her use of the bike? Suddenly he strode away and she sat there watching the bike vibrating urgently beneath her.

He had gone to get his horse and in a moment he had mounted and was galloping off across the plain. The bike put-putted, and Frazer was in pursuit. He didn't look back once, but of course he could hear her following, over the rough and trackless ground, around the curve of a ridge. Now there were ironstone pebbles, sheeny in the sun, a line of trees that followed a watercourse. He made for the trees and rode along by the river and Frazer followed. The water was low, and she spied only one decent hole before he reined in under some coolibahs and dismounted.

Frazer skidded to a halt, left her bike and followed him on foot, glad of her boots. How would it have been in the pretty sandals Aunt Helen liked to see her wearing? He was climbing a slope where there was a bit of low scrub and a few low twisted trees. Frazer caught a glimpse of red earth – desert sandstone! – and her heart pounded and she had to stop herself from slowing down to watch every step she took. On ground like this you could walk on an opal stone and never even know it – if you didn't keep your eyes skinned. But she was going to have plenty of time for that later. Right now, all she needed to know was where that shaft was. 'Here,' she thought, as she followed Jay Dexter – 'here my father trod. Here he found stones that set him thinking. Here if he had lived he would have found his heart's desire.'

The man ahead of her stopped and now he turned and stood waiting for her.

'There's your shaft, Kate,' he said as she came level with him. She hated the familiar way he called her Kate – as if she were a child. Yet because she had said her name was Dwight and it wasn't, she couldn't bring herself to insist, 'Miss Dwight from you, please.'

The shaft was barely discernible. It was grown over with rough prickly scrub and grasses, and it was half filled in with mullock. *He* had done that, she supposed. But there were still mounds of mullock around – red and pink earth showing where nothing had grown. All that was left to show where her father's hidden Aladdin's cave had been. She was biting hard on her lip to keep herself from tears when the man beside her said sardonically, 'Well, what do you think of it? Is it a story?'

It was a story – a story deep in her heart, a story it would choke her to begin to tell him. Frazer turned away a little as she raised her head – to hide her tell-tale face. To her surprise, she could glimpse the homestead in its grove of trees on the slope of the ridge. So the Dexters had been that close – but too unfriendly to care whether a man lived or died. He had asked to be taken to the doctor, but it had been too much trouble – until it was too late. Frazer looked back at Jay Dexter and wondered if he ever felt guilt – or if he had forgotten. That arrogant head, that – patronizing contempt. She knew now that her determination to come here was no longer simply zeal for the opal, belief in her father's belief, a need to follow his dream. It was a positive action against Jay Dexter. She would come and camp on his land and she would stay just as long as she liked. She would let him feel her hatred. But she would be safe as her father had not been, because she would have Caryl and Robert with her, she wouldn't be alone.

She didn't know how many seconds had elapsed since he had asked, 'Is it a story?' but now she told him tensely, 'Where opals are concerned – and people – there's always a story, Mr. Dexter.'

His almost black eyes widened slightly and he moved his head sharply. He said, 'You must be a girl with a great imagination. You should go far with your journalistic career, Kate. Send me a copy of the *Star* when your – story – comes out, will you?' Already he was walking back down the slope and she followed him.

She said to his back, 'If you'd tried to help, I might. But you haven't, have you?'

'No? I showed you the shaft. What else did you expect?'

'Nothing,' said Frazer, and added, 'From you.' She spoke rudely and she saw from his stiffened shoulders that he was annoyed. He turned his head.

'Maybe you'd like to peg out a claim for yourself. That would be one way of getting a story, but you'd find it a high price to pay, I can tell you. You'd pretty soon be tired of it.'

Frazer came level with him. 'Do you know – I just might do that, Mr. Dexter,' she told him with a bright look that suggested he had put the idea into her head at that very minute. 'It sounds quite an idea.' They reached the coolibahs and she got on to the bike and without another word started it up and raced back to the homestead and her aunt's car.

It took her over five hours to drive back to the big country town of Mingari where she lived with the Dwights. The road for most of the way wasn't good, but there was practically no traffic and she drove fast. She had got her driver's licence while she was at boarding school in Sydney. She had good road sense, and quick reflexes, and as she drove she did a lot of thinking and planning. In two weeks, she would have everything ready

15

– camping gear, tools, cooking equipment, clothes. She would write to Caryl tomorrow and set a definite date. Caryl Hill had been her friend at school, though even to Caryl she had never talked about her personal life – the life when she had lived on the opal fields. Caryl was pretty and red-haired, and she had been rather naughty at school though somehow her escapades were always forgiven. Her parents were wealthy hotel people who lived mostly in Sydney but moved round a lot and hadn't a great deal of time for their children, so that Caryl was at boarding school, Robert at a university college. Caryl was going to have a free year before she decided on any kind of a career – and goodness knows what that would be! 'I'll get married,' she always told Frazer.

Frazer had no thoughts about marrying. She didn't know any boys, and anyhow, her head was full of the excitement of opal mining. She had actually tried to per-suade her uncle – it was no use trying to persuade Aunt Helen! – that she could eventually become a buyer. Even an international buyer. He was almost as firm in the view as Aunt Helen that it was unthinkable for a girl to work on the fields amongst rough men. Nevertheless, Frazer told Caryl what she had told nobody else – that next year she intended to go outback and gouge for opals. Caryl had pounced on the idea with screams of delight.

'Fraze! But how fantastic! Let me come too – you must!'

Frazer was not at all certain. She had never talked about her father or about her own past, at school – not even to Caryl. And the plan she had for going to Wanda-lilli was completely private. She was pretty certain her uncle would never let her go off on her own, however, and it was the fact that Caryl said persuasively that her brother would come too that decided her to say yes. You needed a man along if you were going to mine, of course. It was a bad thing to be alone in a shaft – particularly on a place like Wandalilli where the owners of the cattle station were so unfriendly. Frazer had met Caryl's brother Robert a couple of times at school prizegivings.

He was a stolid, respectable, reliable-looking young man, not in the least like his lively sister. He had just finished an Economics course at university, but he wasn't yet starting work. In May, the Hills were all taking off for a year in Europe, and until that time Caryl and Robert were free to do as they pleased. So—

'Okay,' Frazer told Caryl, 'you and Robert can come too. We'll wait till summer's about over.'

She was very certain that she would find the patch of precious opal her father had reckoned he was getting on to, including, she felt in her bones, the gem stone that she would name the Wandalilli Princess, because that's what he would have called it. It might take a long time, it might take a couple of weeks, and then – she didn't know what happened then. She might be lucky and meet a man who was as crazy about opals as her father had been, and they would marry and go prospecting for new fields and – make their fortune.

Frazer had dared to express her ideas very cautiously to Uncle Frank, whom she found more understanding and sympathetic than Aunt Helen, her mother's sister, and he had listened and then said seriously, 'Do you know what I think you're aiming to do, Cathleen? You want to bring back the world of your childhood and make it your life. It won't work, you know. Things change. You're not a child now, you'll see everything with different eyes.'

'I won't,' Frazer had denied passionately. 'I *won't*.' He couldn't understand, because he'd never lived with opals – with the marvellous excitement of the search, the ever-present hope of striking gem stuff. He'd never known what it was to bring the stones to the light out of the earth's darkness – to see breathtaking colour flashing from grey potch, from lifeless dirt. Palaces of fire, shining flames—

But he had said eventually, 'Righto, have a bash at it. Get it out of your system. I'll stand by you, and when it's over we'll talk seriously about your future.'

It was he who had persuaded Aunt Helen to consent too. 'Let the girl go. It's something she's got to do.'

'If you could only grow *up*, Cathleen,' Aunt Helen said when she and Frazer were alone. She had never had a child, and would much have preferred her niece to be conventional and biddable. Right from the first, when Frazer came to live with them at the age of fourteen, Aunt Helen had been a little afraid of Frazer – aggressive, half wild, blunt, without artifice – she had accused her of being all those things. Looking after her had been – yes, rather like feeding a tiger. Aunt Helen had never ventured too close. After a very few months Frazer, instead of attending school in Mingari, was sent away to boarding school in Sydney. Her father had done well enough on the opal fields to finance *that* – which proved conclusively that he was not the 'mad impractical dreamer with a chip on his shoulder' that Aunt Helen called him. Always adding, 'Frances should never have married him. If he'd really loved her, he'd have gone away and let her forget him.'

So now – Frazer's plan was being more or less sanctioned – more or less, because she never mentioned Wandalilli and it was taken for granted she would go to one of the well-known fields, and not alone. But she knew that both her aunt and uncle hoped that she would change her mind before summer was over. Aunt Helen had taken her to Sydney after Christmas, and they had gone to shows and concerts, bought clothes, and eaten at the best restaurants and met nice people, Aunt Helen's friends and their children. Frazer had pleased her aunt by proving that she could behave herself admirably.

'You do have good breeding, and it shows through, though I'm surprised they didn't knock off a few more of the rough edges at school.'

Sydney with Aunt Helen was a kind of crash course in manners and social know-how, and on the whole Frazer was bored by it. Then it was home to Mingari and a trial period working on the newspaper.

'Anyhow,' she thought with a feeling of relief as she drove the long miles home from Wandalilli, 'all that is just about finished.' Her real life was about to begin. And she wasn't going to tell them she was heading straight for Wandalilli. She would pretend she was going to White Cliffs.

'Stick to the fields,' Uncle Frank had said. 'Stick to the old diggings. It's not safe to wander around the Corner Country if you don't know the tanks. And keep in touch, Cathleen.'

That was what they both said to her two weeks later when she set off on her loaded motorbike, complete with tent and all sorts of gear you needed when you went gouging for opals in the outback. 'Keep in touch, Cathleen, and see that you and Caryl and Robert stick with the other fossickers. Don't go off on your own where there's no water, and no one to lend you a hand if you need it.'

Frazer promised yes to everything, and then she was speeding off on her own, through Mingari, and out along the long straight road that crossed the empty sunlit plains.

Some hours later she reached Minning Minning, the outback town where she was to meet Caryl and Robert. There she purchased various odds and ends, including a pick and a shovel, a gas cylinder for camp cooking, and a supply of food. This accomplished, she went to the motel restaurant and ordered herself an iced lemonade, and sat drinking it by the window where she could watch the street. The Hills were taking the train to Burke and coming on from there by motorbike, Caryl riding pillion. Frazer's thighs were aching a little from the long run. She had removed her helmet and slung her jacket over the back of the chair and was cooling down in her black jeans and short-sleeved mulberry sweater – not the sort of gear Aunt Helen liked at all!

It seemed a long while before at last a motorbike came down the wider rather empty street and braked to a stop outside the motel. Frazer dashed out of the restaurant to welcome the two helmeted figures just as Caryl climbed from the pillion.

'Fraze! We've got here at last! Isn't it marvellous? But

19

I'm just so steamed up in all these clothes, and a wreck from all that ghastly time in the train! I never knew Australia was so big and so empty.'

Frazer was staring at the man who had dismounted and was now standing beside Caryl. Robert was fairish, chunky and solid. *This* man had a dark beard and moustache, and longish dark hair, and he was decidedly stringy. And his eyes were a peculiarly light grey.

'Oh,' Caryl said, her green eyes laughing, mischievous. 'Introductions. This is Rex Byfield, Frazer. Rex – Frazer Madigan.'

'Hello,' said Rex. He looked hard and curiously at Frazer as though he were summing her up, and she felt decidedly disconcerted. A boy-friend was somehow very different from a brother, and she knew that her own 'Hello' didn't sound terribly enthusiastic.

'I'll explain later about Robert,' Caryl said airily. 'What's the restaurant like? I'm dying of thirst! Are we staying here, at the motel? It looks quite modern! Unexpected in a place like this.' She was full of excitement, her cheeks flushed, her eyes bright under the helmet which she now pulled off, tossing back her bright red hair.

They all went into the restaurant and ordered cold drinks. Frazer, now she saw Rex without his helmet, had the sinking feeling that she wasn't going to like him much. It was partly his eyes, partly the way he looked at her – cold, speculative, as though she were an object rather than a human being. He asked across his tall glass of Coke, 'Are we really going to dig for opals or is it all a bit of a joke, *Fraze*?'

She coloured at the way he said her name and told him flatly, '*I'm* digging for opals. Why did you come along?'

'We want to find opals too,' Caryl said. 'I can hardly wait. I'm sure Rex will find some and become fabulously rich, and Daddy will do a double take.'

Rex continued to watch Frazer.

'Exactly where do we look?' he wanted to know. 'If we're not going to White Cliffs – do we work from here?

Make daily forages, as it were?'

'No,' said Frazer shortly. He sounded so scathing – as though he didn't believe she knew a thing about it. 'I've got a place picked out. And we're camping.' She looked at Caryl. 'Didn't you bring a tent? I told you when I wrote—'

'Of course we have tents, Fraze,' said Caryl placatingly. 'But this motel does look nice – and so cool. It's *hot* outside.'

'Summer's over,' said Frazer. 'It's not all that hot. And it would be stupid to stay in Minning Minning. There's a beauty spot by the river where we can camp. This place we're making for is on a cattle station where there's an old shaft.'

Rex looked more scathing than ever. 'Raking over some old place that's been abandoned? Where's the sense?'

Frazer asked him coldly, 'Have you ever been fossicking – or mining?'

His light grey eyes looked at her stonily. 'Actually no. I've done most things, but not that. Have you?'

'Actually, yes,' said Frazer. 'And I've got good reasons for going to Wandalilli.'

'Such as?'

'I don't need to tell you. If you don't want to come along then you don't have to.'

'Frazer!' exclaimed Caryl, laughing a little. 'Don't take it like that. Of course we want to come along—'

'I wish—' Frazer stopped abruptly. It was no use wishing Robert had come instead of Rex. Robert hadn't come and she would have to make the best of it. It was just a pity she didn't like Caryl's boy-friend. Perhaps when she got to know him better she would change her mind about him. As it was, she simply couldn't think what Caryl saw in him. She sighed a little. 'I suppose you can use a pick, Rex.'

'Sure I can use a pick. I've worked on the roads before this. I'm not a poet.'

'That's a break. You should be *some* use then.'

'Thanks for nothing,' he retorted, and they eyed each other inimically. Caryl was beginning to look a little bit upset, and Frazer felt a pang of remorse. She must really like Rex. 'But I'll bet her folks don't,' reflected Frazer shrewdly. And that could be why he was here now. Frazer just hoped he was not going to spoil everything, that this wasn't going to become some kind of amorous escapade instead of an opal prospecting venture.

For a moment she wished she could have come on her own ...

When they reached Wandalilli it was almost sundown. They didn't have to go too near the homestead. Frazer had calculated that if they followed the line of trees along the river bed they would reach the flats down from the old shaft without fail, and that was what they did. She explained carelessly to the others, 'It's all okay – we've got our licences, and I've seen the people who own the place. They won't bother us.'

They rode quietly along by the river with Frazer in the lead, and the dying sun made a gilded pool of the plain spread out before them, streaked here and there with the long finger strokes of tree shadows. They saw some of Jay Dexter's stock moving slowly, gilded too, glorified by the sun, and then Frazer caught sight of the low slope of the ridge where her father, Lee Madigan, had sunk his last shaft.

She put on pace and rode ahead suddenly, turned her bike in a long slow sweep, and pulled up on flat ground sheltered by big eucalyptus. This would be the place to camp, with the river close enough to fetch water from it, and that hole not so far away where they could bathe. There was a bit of low scrub around, but enough cleared space to pitch their tents without problems. Steadying herself with one foot, she waited for the others to join her. The sun fell below the horizon, the golden colours vanished, and it was suddenly almost dark. On a distant rise, a yellow light appeared in Wandalilli homestead. 'I'm here,' Frazer said inwardly to the image of Jay Dexter that had somehow imposed itself on her mind. 'So how do you like that?' Then deliberately, she turned away from that yellow light.

The others had arrived by now, and Caryl sat on the pillion seat, her arms clasped around Rex's waist, staring around, her green eyes alight. 'It's romantic – but just a little bit scary. I'm glad *you're* with us, Rex. Are we really going to camp here – sleep here all night?'

'Of course,' Frazer said. 'And there's nothing to be scared of. Even without Rex,' she almost added, but forbore. After all, he was Caryl's hero ... She got off her bike and began to unload her camping gear. Rex, who seemed inclined to ignore her since their little brush in the restaurant, began unloading too, while Caryl moved off to explore before it was completely dark.

They had got two of the tiny tents up when a car came across the plain, its headlights making Frazer blink momentarily. She felt her heartbeats quicken. This would be Jay Dexter – coming to welcome them, she thought sarcastically. He would certainly get a surprise to find her here! He braked his car uncomfortably close and left the headlights shining, and then from a world that was almost completely dark he came striding towards them. Out of the corner of her eye, Frazer saw Caryl slip back into the scrub from which she had been emerging.

She felt a strange shock of recognition as her eyes focussed on Jay Dexter. Without his hat, his thick shock of black hair gave him a kind of savage look, so that she shivered slightly.

'What the hell are you two doing here?' he demanded. He evidently hadn't seen Caryl, and he was concentrating on Rex, long-haired, bearded – one of the 'undesirable types' with their mining licences coming on to his property. But Frazer was sure he'd have acted the same even if it had been the stocky conventional Robert instead. It was she who answered him, her eyes fiery bright, 'We're pitching our tents, Mr. Dexter. We've got mining rights and we're going to look for opals on your land.'

He swung towards her abruptly as she spoke, and stared, taking in her slim figure in the black jeans and mulberry shirt, her gold-streaked hair flattened by the red crash helmet that lay shining on the ground.

'So it's Cathleen Dwight,' he said drawlingly, and plainly completely amazed.

'Yes, it is. I took up your suggestion, you see. Do you want to take a look at our licences?'

He glanced at Rex and then back at her and his lip curled slightly. 'Don't bother,' he said coolly. 'I'll take you on trust.' She could see contempt in his eyes, and it occurred to her suddenly that he must think she and Rex were here alone. Well, he could think what he liked, and whether they were or not was not his concern. 'However,' he continued, 'you might remember you don't have the right to spread yourself all over my paddocks. Right here is where you stay – and up at the shaft. I presume you mean to mess around there. You can use the river water, but remember to boil it before you drink it. I don't want you sick ... Don't disturb my stock, and don't leave any gates open. Though you shouldn't have occasion to open any gates till you're leaving. Which I hope will be soon,' he finished pleasantly. 'Now you' – with a gesture of his head in Frazer's direction – 'you instigated this. You can come along with me up to the homestead and we'll get a few facts straightened out. I like to get things quite clear with any fossickers who happen to wander on to Wanda-lilli.' He gave a grim-looking smile, his teeth shining whitely.

Frazer had stiffened. They had their miners' rights, so what else was there to get straightened out? What facts did he want? Instead of refusing point blank to obey him, she said coldly, 'We haven't eaten yet.'

His eyebrows ascended. 'Your mate here can get on with warming up the baked beans in your absence,' he said.

Frazer blinked. They probably were going to have baked beans tonight, and his remark somehow and quite ludicrously took the wind out of her sails. Before she could think of a retort Rex, who was leaving her to it and had started stowing some of the gear in the tents, told her

24

carelessly, 'Go ahead – *Cathleen*. I'll carry on like the gentleman says.'

Frazer looked around helplessly for Caryl, but she had completely vanished. She was obviously keeping out of the way and Frazer didn't blame her.

'Come along now, Kate,' said Jay Dexter, and he took her not only firmly, but quite roughly by the arm, and whether she liked it or not, she was steered towards the Land Rover.

CHAPTER TWO

THE minute he was seated beside her, she asked icily, 'What facts do you want to get straightened out? We could do it just as well at the camp here.'

'We could. But as I'm saving face for you, Cathleen Dwight, you might try and be grateful for it.' She had no idea what he was talking about, but he said nothing further till he had started up the motor. Then as they drove through the darkness where shadows of trees and beasts and long dry grasses wove eerie patterns that moved in the headlights, he elaborated further. 'You're up to something, aren't you? Does your uncle know you're camping out with that fellow? Or shall I persuade you to ring up from the homestead and tell him exactly what's going on? And then we'll decide whether or not you'd better sleep under my roof tonight instead of out in the bush.'

Frazer's heart had begun to pound angrily. So that was why he was dragging her off to the homestead, was it? Well, she wasn't here alone with Rex, and if she had been then it was absolutely nothing to do with him. She told him with mock patience, 'My uncle knows I've gone fossicking for opals, and he knows who I'm with. In fact he knows all about it.' She paused and frowned slightly, because she wasn't really telling the truth. Her uncle thought she was at White Cliffs with Caryl and Robert Hill. However, she was under no obligation to tell Jay Dexter that, so she continued flatly, 'In any case – for your information I'm not here alone with Rex – my girl friend Caryl is here too. She just didn't happen to be around when you appeared.'

'You expect me to believe that?' he demanded, with a piercing sideways glance.

'Why not? You can find out if it's true or not if you go back to the camp. So you see, there's no need for anyone

26

to ring my uncle. It's all perfectly straightforward. We're fossickers and we're going to see what we can find in that old mine.'

He was driving slowly now, apparently thinking over what she had said, and then he pulled up, but left the engine running, and turned to face her in the faint light of the dashboard.

'That I find just too hard to swallow, Kate. Why here – where no one's ever found a thing?'

She looked back at him, her eyes guarded. 'How would you know? People don't shout out about their finds if they have any sense.'

'No. But if they find something they come back.'

Frazer said, 'If they're still alive.' And then she began to shiver. It was not simply because the night was turning coolish, but because there was something about actually being with Jay Dexter, who had done *that* to her father, that made her shiver.

'So you've come to bug me, have you?' he said after a long minute during which his glance had not wavered. 'You're still determined to get a story. Have you been listening to tales – rumours – on the opal fields?' Frazer didn't answer, and he continued, 'I'll guarantee your uncle doesn't know what you're up to. What did you tell him? That you were going to Lightning Ridge – to White Cliffs?'

She had, but she certainly wasn't going to admit it to him. 'My uncle's not as – suspicious and distrustful as you. Do you think I'm a child that he'd ask me for a complete blueprint of my plans?'

'A moment ago,' he said dryly, 'you told me that he knew the lot. Certainly if you were *my* niece I'd want details, and even then I'm not sure I wouldn't come along too. You're not much more than a child, by the look of you. Could be still at school. I'd say you were seventeen or eighteen at the most and young for your age. I take it you live in Mingari with these relatives of yours?'

'Yes,' Frazer admitted, then wished immediately that she had refused to answer a personal question. She was annoyed by his attitude, and she wasn't a young eighteen. She had seen more of life – real life – at the age of fourteen than most of the other girls at school had seen at seventeen, and one day she would tell him that – one day before she left Wandalilli. But not now.

His eyes had narrowed and he appeared to be making up his mind about something. Finally he said, 'I'm not at all sure I shouldn't get in touch with Frank Dwight. I'll take your word for it there's another girl with you, but—'

'But what?' exclaimed Frazer angrily. 'Do you think I'm – I'm sleeping with Rex or something? Because I'm not. And anyhow, he's Caryl's friend, and we're here for the reason I told you.'

'And I damn well can't see why you've come here. I promise you most faithfully it won't pay off in any way at all. You took me seriously when I tossed you that challenge the other day, did you? Well, I didn't mean you to in any sense. You won't get a story – you won't even experience anything worth writing about, and you certainly won't find any opals. So it won't pay off in any way at all.'

Frazer shrugged. 'How would you know?' She didn't want a story, but he could think that if he liked, and she hoped it would make him uneasy. And she *was* going to find opal because her father had mined opal all his life and he had been positive he was getting on to something good on Wandalilli. He had believed it with every fibre of his being. It was only death that had robbed him of seeing his dream come true. There were a number of things that Jay Dexter didn't know, for all his infuriating superiority.

'Kate,' he told her positively now, 'I do know.' He put a hand on her knee and she flinched as though she had been burnt.

'Don't touch me!'

She saw his dark eyebrows go up and she heard his exasperated sigh. He removed his hand and told her, 'All right, we won't use the telephone. But I'm going to keep an eye on you all the same – and a pretty strict one. So just don't get up to any tricks.' She saw him move to put the Land Rover in gear and she opened the door quickly and slid out.

'I'll walk back. I'd rather. If you want to check that Caryl's there you can drive down on your own.' She slammed the door shut and turned away and started running across the dark uneven ground of the paddock towards the tents. She didn't know why, but she had to get away from him – there was something unnerving about being shut up in the car with him . . .

Rex had lighted a lamp and she could see he had put up the third tent now. Well, that might convince Jay Dexter. Evidently it did, because he got the car going and drove straight on towards the homestead.

Frazer slowed down. She was breathing fast, and it wasn't only because she had been running. So that was Dexter – her father's enemy, and now her enemy. And he was going to keep a strict eye on her. Well, that would be a change, seeing he didn't generally seem to care what happened to fossickers on his land. Though no doubt by keeping an eye on her he meant he would seize the first possible opportunity to get her and Caryl and Rex off his property. If he could. Because Frazer simply wasn't going until she had found her father's – and her own – dream.

It was a funny thing, but her head, that should tonight have been full of the excitement of at last being here – for she had thought of this and nothing else to the detriment of her schooling for a long long time now – her head was full of Jay Dexter, and mixed up with her hatred of him, her antagonism and defiance, her knowledge that because he had not cared her father had died, was something else that she couldn't understand. At school, her thoughts of the future had been so uncomplicated, so clear. Now— Well, it was like finding an opal and discovering it had a sand spot running into it, spoiling its perfection. Or that it had a film of potch across it that might – or might not – mean that it wouldn't face up into a gem of lovely, lively, flashing colours . . .

When she got back to the others, she told them, '*That's* over. I got that sorted out pretty quickly.'

Caryl, who had found a tin of baked beans and was emptying them into the pan, said, 'Good. And Fraze, I hope I did the right thing. I nearly rushed out and said Boo, but he sounded so cranky I thought I'd better keep out of the way.'

Rex, sitting on one of the camp-stools and smoking, wasn't so easily satisfied. He asked, 'What did you get sorted out – Cathleen Dwight?'

'Oh yes,' Caryl looked up with a mischievous grin. 'Why did he call you that, Frazer?'

'Because I sometimes use that name,' said Frazer untruthfully, reddening as she spoke. 'My name *is* Cathleen and – and Dwight is handy because people know then I'm connected with Uncle Frank and the *Mingari Star.*'

'Won't wash,' commented Rex laconically.

Frazer gave him a cold look. 'All right, I told him that was my name for reasons that are personal and private. So now will you mind your own business?'

'When you've told us what you got sorted out. Or was that personal and private too? I notice you didn't get all the way to the homestead.'

Frazer flushed scarlet. She said furiously, 'You have a nasty mind like some other men. He just wanted to make sure I wasn't going to write up anything for the paper, that's all. Station owners don't always like publicity – he doesn't want to have a rush of fossickers on his place.'

'So he couldn't have sorted that out while I was listening?'

'Oh, stop sparring, you two;' entreated Caryl. 'Let's eat. I'm famished. Just let Frazer alone, Rex.'

'Gladly,' said Rex. He got up from the stool and went to stand beside Caryl, cupped her chin in his hand, tilted her pretty face and kissed her on the lips.

Frazer, who had never been kissed, never had a boy-friend, turned away embarrassed. That way, she was not grown up – and didn't particularly want to be.

Next morning she was up just after dawn, itching to have a look at the shaft, because she had dreamed of it and of her father, and the dream had been so real she had wept when she woke from it.

Still in the shelter of the tent, and knowing it would be coolish outside – she had spent the greater part of her life on opal fields and she knew the outback – she pulled on her black jeans, her mulberry shirt and her jacket, and then she wriggled outside with her boots. Before she zipped them up she straightened to look at the world. It was empty and beautiful. There was a pale, pale sky above that would deepen to cerulean and then to heavenly blue as the day grew hot. There was a red glow in the east and a burst of dazzling light that hurt her eyes. Long shadows reached across the pink of the dried grasses, the leaves of the coolibahs caught the light. Galahs shrieked in the trees by the river and a pair of a sacred kingfishers sped like azure spearheads through the morning sky. Up above, three kookaburras sat on a bough and began the low and tentative 'koo – koo – koo' that was a preliminary to bursts of weird laughter. Further off, some cattle moved slowly, their dark hides touched with red, and further still, if she turned slightly she could see the station homestead in its green oasis. She had been only as far as the verandah of that homestead and she wondered vaguely what it was like inside. And she wondered about the woman she had met there. Jay Dexter's wife? Had she been here when Lee Madigan had pitched his tent and sunk his shaft? No, Frazer couldn't believe she had been. A woman would have shown more concern. And the Old Man – was he still there?

Frazer stooped, impatient with her own throughts, and zipped up her boots. She had no intention of thinking about the Dexters.

She left the shelter of the trees and made her way in the direction of the slope. It was strange how old habits returned when you were in the right sort of country. Already Frazer had her eyes skinned watching for stones that might possibly contain colour. She stopped three or four times on her way up to the shaft to pick up a fragment and examine it, then toss it down when there was no glassy shine. The gently sloping hillside was rough with patches of stiff grass and low shrubs, but here and there the red desert sandstone showed through – sandstone that capped opal dirt that might yield treasure. Yet it wasn't the treasure that was the real lure. It was the beauty, the thrill of finding those imprisoned palaces of fire, and Frazer remembered how she and her father had hated having to sell their finds . . .

She reached the old mine and stood staring down at it, her mind whirling with emotions and images garnered from the past; that belonged in a life that for her had ended when she was fourteen years old and had been sent away to live with her mother's sister.

She sat down on a rock, not yet sun-warmed, and stared at the scrub that had grown up and almost covered the logs her father had put around the mouth of the shaft; at the mullock he had shovelled out with hours of hard, patient work – and that someone had since shovelled back in again. Jay Dexter, no doubt. She thought of her father's burning enthusiasm and personal warmth, of how he had called her his Princess and let her help him on the opal fields from when she was six years old and her mother had died. For Frazer, that life had been the accepted way of living, and she had been happy. Her father had always worked for himself, lovingly though hard, using his hands the way men had done before him for years and years. He and Frazer had lived roughly, simply, but life had been exciting and for Frazer beyond criticism. Her father had been her ideal, and she saw things through his eyes and believed implicitly in his judgments. Her hair cut short, wearing dungarees and later, jeans, going to school with the other miners' children, she had been her father's mate, his little Trojan. And when they were alone at night, eating their dinner and later sorting stones, she was his little Princess.

Princess of the Shining Flame – that was one of the names he had in mind for *the* Opal when he found it – and

32

then he and she would live like kings, and who knew where they would travel together? But they would always come back to the opal fields where their love and their work belonged. She didn't know why he called her Frazer instead of Cathleen, though she suspected later it was possibly because he preferred her to be taken for a boy. And as Frazer, with her short tawny hair and her often torn, always dirty jeans, she worked around the mine, helped haul up the buckets, went down the shaft to go through the dirt he had loosened with his pick. She had liked the rough work. She didn't want to confine herself to sorting and classing the stones and facing the better ones on her jeweller's lathe, though that was thrilling work, suited to her sensitive fingers and feminine mind, her father used to say. Sometimes he had a mate working with him, and then Frazer would regret she wasn't a boy, that she had a girl's limitations and simply couldn't achieve what a man could do.

It had been one of these mates who had been the reason for her idyllic life coming to an end. He was a young man called Dave who had come to the opal fields for a month's holiday, hoping to make a fortune for himself. Her father had taken him on, because he was so completely inexperienced, and Lee happened to need help at that particular time. Lee had pegged out a claim in a new place and he was putting down a shaft with the usual optimistic hope of bottoming on opal, and he was quite specific that fourteen-year-old Frazer was not going to do any 'navvying'. That was probably because he had had another letter from Aunt Helen telling him it was time something was done about 'Frances's daughter'.

'She means you should go to a school for young ladies and live in a proper house, Princess,' Lee had said, and Frazer had snorted and said she didn't want to go to a ladies' college, and that it would kill her to live in a proper house. At fourteen, she was well developed physically, tallish as she had always been, and decidedly feminine in the curves that were revealed by her tee-shirts and tight-fitting jeans. Lee was worried about her, undecided.

'Maybe I should send you to Mingari. Helen's always been willing to have you – even though she's never forgiven me for marrying her sister. And Frank Dwight's a decent bloke. You wouldn't have to live on them, we've money enough and a couple of good parcels of stones I could sell right now—'

It only needed Frazer to say passionately, 'Dad, *no*! I couldn't bear to leave you,' and he was reassured.

That was until Dave came. And right from the first, Dave watched Frazer who couldn't keep away from the shaft and from picking over the mullock that was heaved out – in case something should be missed, because you just never knew. She wondered why her father was so irritable, why he nagged at her to get back to the wheel and 'face those we picked out the other night' – just as soon as she was home from school and turned up at the shaft. She found out why when he was away one day and she came up and found Dave alone. He had put his hands on her and tried to kiss her, and Frazer had yelled blue murder. Not that Dave was vicious or anything like it, but she was only fourteen and not the least little bit sexually precocious.

That was the finish. Her father took her to Mingari two days later.

Frazer shifted slightly on her stone on the hillside beside the partly filled-in shaft, her violet eyes sombre. She wished now she hadn't screamed when Dave had touched her. It had been purely instinctive. She was quite certain a kiss would have done her no harm. That way, she wouldn't have left her father and—

And everything would have been different. He wouldn't have gone away prospecting on his own, he wouldn't have come to Wandalilli where his presence was resented. He wouldn't have had to depend on people who didn't care, or who didn't believe in his pain, when he was ill.

She remembered the last time she had ever seen him when he had come to Sydney to sell a parcel of stones to pay for her schooling – and to see her and take her out for

34

the afternoon. He had been dressed up in a suit and looking almost conventional, almost smart, and because she had so seldom seen him looking like that, he had seemed almost a stranger at first. He had been limping.

'I had an accident with the pick,' he had explained. 'I've told you Old Man Dexter and his son don't like my being on their land, and they haven't tried to hide it, but my foot needed attention and I went up to the homestead and asked for a ride into town to see the doctor. But not on your life! That was too much trouble. If I came to grief that was my look-out – they'd never invited me there. Wrapped up in themselves and their own importance – like all the station people it's ever been my misfortune to meet.'

'And they wouldn't help you, Dad?' Frazer was appalled. 'But your foot – has it healed? Is it—'

'Hold your horses, honey. The young fellow put a few stitches in it,' her father said with a grimace. 'It'll be all right.'

Frazer had shuddered. No anaesthetic, of course – as though her father were unfeeling, or – or like an animal. She had squeezed his arm sympathetically. 'Watch it doesn't turn septic, Dad. Oh, I wish I were there to dress it for you! Couldn't I—'

'Honey, you couldn't. It's no place for you with no friends around, and I tell you they'd get rid of me if they could. If there was one gallon of water left in the dam, they'd let their precious cattle trample over my dying body to get at it first ... But I'm staying, and be damned to them, because I'm on to something this time, Princess. Really on to something. This is *it*. I'm within a hair's breadth of achieving my dream – our dream. I feel it in my bones. I've always known when opal was near. Opal and I – we warm to each other. And this time it's really opal. Each blow I strike, each shovelful of dirt I lift out of that drive – I feel it there waiting, reaching through to me, sending me its tiny urgent whispers. I'll lift my Shining Flame, my Wandalilli Princess, from its cradle in the dark earth and hold it for the sun to see and to envy—'

Listening to him then, seeing the light that burned in his blue eyes, how she had thrilled! She had known that what he said was true and she had loved the way he told it. Even the fact that he had enemies to fight – the hated Dexters – had seemed to add a touch of nobility to his struggle. She didn't once see her father as a rather shabby dreamer with a stubborn mouth – she saw a knight seeking an ideal.

Three weeks later he was dead. He had died just after reaching hospital, too late for an operation. The headmistress had called Frazer in to her study to break the news to her only the day after she received the last letter he ever wrote. She had been worried about him already, but she had never dreamed this would happen. He had written, 'I've had some bad abdominal pains the last twenty-four hours, darling – could be appendicitis. But don't worry – I can get myself over to the homestead, and that I shall do the minute I seal up this letter. I'll get them to take me to town to the doctor right away. That's a promise, so *don't worry*. It's too bad it should happen right now, when my Wandalilli Princess is almost in my hands. How do I know? The old intuition – the sympathy that exists between me and the most beautiful stone in the world ...'

For Frazer, the shock of his death had been acute. She didn't know when it had come home to her that the station people hadn't taken him to the doctor when he asked. They hadn't taken him for two days. A man in bad pain. It had been too much trouble, she had thought bitterly. And she had wondered if the son, Jay Dexter, had tried out some bush remedy on him. She had felt a burning futile anger and hatred for the Dexters. And despite them, she had vowed that she would continue her father's search the minute she left school.

Despite them? Hadn't it been just a little bit as if that way she would be striking a blow at them?

Yes, she would follow the star that had beckoned and beguiled Lee Madison and that he had been cheated of attaining at the eleventh hour. Meanwhile, she had to finish her schooling. Her father had, before returning to Wandalilli, handed over to the Dwights the bulk of his money to pay for that, and to Frazer herself he had given what was to prove a final gift – two stones he had found when she was eleven and that she had believed he had sold years ago.

'And now here I am at last,' thought Frazer from her seat on the gentle hillside. She wondered if the stones would warm to her, when she and Caryl and Rex had shovelled the mullock out of the shaft and she could go on where her father had left off, gentling her way along under the ironstone band that topped the opal dirt.

One thing she knew. She had to do it – for reasons that merged into each other inextricably. For her father's sake and to satisfy the deep urge that had been born and fostered in her . . .

The day was unfolding now and soon Rex and Caryl would be up. She made her way back to the camp and put a billy of water to boil on the tiny gas cooker. They would light a fire later if they needed it. The sun was growing warm and she tossed her jacket aside and sat on one of the camp stools, the mugs stacked near her on the ground.

'We need a box,' she thought, and remembered with a pang the weirdly assorted tables she had shared with her father in days gone by – cross-cut logs, flat rocks, packing cases – anything had done. Though they had a real table at home.

She had got up to toss a handful of tea-leaves into the billy when a shadow fell across the ground and she looked up to see Dexter there watching her.

'So you're the one who gets up first, are you?' he commented. 'I thought it might have been the boy-friend.'

'Well, it's not the boy-friend, it's me,' said Frazer. She looked at him levelly, and she wondered if he felt her hatred and was mystified as to the reason for it. Unless maybe he was the sort of man who was used to being hated.

He said after a second, 'You continually amaze me, you modern – liberated I believe is the word – girls. Getting

37

around on your own the minute you leave school, the world your oyster, but no ambition, no feeling of responsibility. Leaving your jobs if you have one. What do your parents – no, I believe you don't have parents, do you? What do your uncle and aunt, then, think of all this? Do they let you play at being a reporter when it suits you, then come out here in the bush in a mixed group, and still sleep with easy minds?'

Frazer said, 'You'd have to ask them about that. But don't get me mixed up with liberated girls. I know exactly what you mean by that.' Her glance strayed worriedly towards the tents as she spoke. She should be rousing up the others now to come and have breakfast, but she just wasn't absolutely sure if they were sleeping in separate tents or not. And if they weren't – well, she didn't want to know, and she didn't want Jay Dexter to know either. The recollection of the way Rex had kissed Caryl last night still troubled her oddly. It gave her a disturbing awareness of the fact that she was in some ways raw and inexperienced herself, though she had always thought at school that *she* was the one who had been around.

Jay Dexter's eyes were on her speculatively as he stood, thumbs hooked into his narrow snakeskin belt, his hat slanted forward over his brows.

'Don't protest too much, Kate,' he advised cynically. 'I'm not saying I have a decided opinion one way or the other about this liberation bit. When it comes to sex – to sleeping with a man – it's a very individual and personal matter and always has been, I'd guess, for the sensitive intelligent type of girl.'

Frazer blinked with embarrassment and stooped to stir the tea with a gum twig. Her cheeks had reddened and she hadn't the least idea what to say. She had no practice whatsoever in this kind of conversation. It had been one thing to burst out her protest at white heat last night in the darkness of the car, but it was quite another thing to stand here in the clear light of the morning and take part in a conversation with a man about – such things. In fact she who had thought she knew so much about the world and about men – for she had met plenty of men in her young life – was now beginning to think she knew very little about either. This dark-skinned man Dexter, sinuous, masculine, self-assured, whose dark eyes made her feel strangely self-conscious, who treated her as if she were neither child nor woman, was completely outside her experience. She couldn't quite decide why he was so different from Uncle Frank – the opal miners – the teachers at the tiny country school she had once attended. But he was, she reminded herself, a wealthy station owner, and towards them she and her father had always felt a natural antipathy – for very personal reasons. It was odd to realize that she was actually related to one – the grandfather who had so ruthlessly banished his daughter from his life because of the man she married. And Frazer couldn't imagine a man kinder and more lovable than her father.

'No comment?' Jay Dexter asked sardonically, and she looked up instinctively, then wished she hadn't, because she met those almost black eyes fully. She wondered just how long she'd been twirling the eucalyptus twig around in the boiling water, and she was quite sure he was laughing at her in a very unkind way – and would go home and tell his wife how amusing it had been tormenting her.

She said bluntly, 'No. I don't want to talk to you. We're going to have breakfast in a minute. Why don't you go home and talk to your wife?'

His wide mouth curved in a half smile and his eyebrows tilted. 'You don't have a very fortunate manner, do you, Kate?' he taunted. 'You'll never make the grade as a reporter, I'm afraid ... As for my wife, I don't happen to have one. I depend for my breakfast conversation and for my – loving – on the occasional liberated girl who finds me sufficiently attractive and sympathetic to form a – temporary alliance.'

Frazer bit her lip and coloured deeply. And wished she could go into her tent. That woman at the homestead, she thought – she hadn't looked *that* sort of a woman—

'It was my sister Barbara you met at the house the

39

other day, by the way,' he said crisply. He had unhooked his thumbs from his belt, produced cigarette papers and tobacco from his pocket, and was rolling himself a cigarette without even looking what he was doing. 'Do you smoke? Or not before breakfast?'

'I don't—' Frazer stopped and amended it hastily, idiotically, 'Not before breakfast, at least.' Why after all shouldn't she confess to not smoking at all? Another part of her mind was taking note of what he had said about that woman at the house. Yes, of course it was his sister, she could see a resemblance now. But he – Jay Dexter – had more vitality, and he was harder – much, much harder. It reminded her of why she hated him, and she hardened too.

Now he commented, 'You're wise. There at any rate. Smoking's a bad habit. I'll give it up myself one of these days. When I marry, maybe.' He grinned a little as if to himself, lit the cigarette and asked her, 'Are you going to wake your friends?'

She bit her lip. Of course, that was why he had come here – to make sure that Caryl really existed. She told him shortly, 'They'll get up when they're ready. I'm not going to rouse them up for you.'

At exactly that moment Caryl emerged from her tent, sleepy-eyed, her red hair tumbled, her boots in her hand. She looked very pretty – and very sexy too. When she saw Jay Dexter, she widened her eyes and exclaimed, 'Oh! I thought it was the other two. Excuse me!' She dropped her boots and smoothed back her hair with her fingers and smiled sleepily at Jay Dexter. Frazer, a little dismayed and nervous, found she was trying to see Caryl through Dexter's eyes. Pretty and aware of it, her brown velvet trousers and embroidered cotton blouse top quality – Frazer glanced swiftly at the man who stood nearby indolently smoking to see if she could gauge his reaction. But his eyes were narrowed and he looked merely thoughtful.

Something was required, so she said, 'This is Caryl Hill.'

He nodded and completed the introductions himself. 'My name's Dexter – Jay Dexter. I suppose you know that you're here on a wild goose chase, Caryl? You don't look like you're dressed for business and you're right. If you really want to play around fossicking for opals, you make for one of the proven fields. You'll meet lots of people like yourself there too.' He paused and then asked dryly, 'Or am I mistaken? You're not here to gauge out opals at all.'

'Oh, we are, Mr. Dexter,' said Caryl, her green eyes wide. 'Frazer – Cathleen knows all about it, and she picked your place. I hope you don't mind? We have our miners' rights and all that sort of thing, and I promise we won't do any harm here, we won't set fire to the bush or anything like that.'

'You'd better not,' he said, obviously not in the least won over by Caryl's manner. 'And I'm sorry, but I'm not prepared to give you a big welcome – any of you. All I hope is that you get it out of your systems quickly.'

Quite abruptly, he moved off. The two girls watched in silence as he strode through the shelter of the tall trees, swung up on to the horse he had left tethered some yards away, and cantered off across the plain. Caryl made a rude face and began to pull on her boots. She remarked, 'He's handsome, but about as friendly as a death adder, isn't he? I wonder if it's worth while working on him.'

'What?' said Frazer, flushing.

'Trying a bit of charm, a bit of gentle persuasion,' said Caryl, her mischievous green eyes thoughtful. 'After all, he's a man, and we're girls. It can work wonders, you know, if you strike the right note. What do you think? Shall we try? It would be funny, wouldn't it, to make him sort of change his tune.'

Frazer shook her head. 'I won't be in it,' she said firmly. She knew that Jay Dexter was not like that. He didn't want them there, and nothing on earth would make him more friendly. 'You'd better wake Rex,' she told Caryl. 'I'm going to mix up some scrambled eggs.'

'In a mo,' said Caryl. She zipped up her boots and came

over to join Frazer who was pouring tea into two of the mugs. 'About Rex,' she said then. 'I hope you like him – I know he's kind of rough, not like the boys your parents like you to meet, with high status jobs and lots of money and the right background and all that kind of thing. I met him at a party – well, I didn't really, I told my parents that.' She helped herself to sugar and stirred it in. 'I was at this party and it was just so boring I walked out and I went into an espresso bar for a drink, and *he* came in and – and lit my cigarette and – we just looked at each other—' She bit her lip and giggled a little. 'It was all so like you read about in stories, I just began to laugh and laugh and so did he. We could see ourselves in a big mirror behind the counter and I was all dressed up in a long party dress that'd cost a packet, and eye make-up and all that sort of thing, and there was he in jeans and one of those awful skinny cotton shirts. And he looked kind of hungry with that beard and his thin face. Actually, I wouldn't be surprised if he came from exactly the same kind of background as us and had rebelled and cleared out. He's never said. Anyhow, we just – we just fell in love with each other.' She raised her tea mug and looked at Frazer soulfully over it.

Frazer said uncomfortably, because Rex didn't appeal to her in the slightest degree, 'What did your family say? Or don't they know?'

'There's nothing to *know*,' said Caryl. 'Of course I asked him home, we have a flat in Edgecliff at the moment, but Mummy wouldn't have anything to do with him and she lectured me for two whole days after. She kept reminding me I was the legal owner of a hotel and when I'm twenty-one I'll have quite a lot of money, so I've got to be careful who I mix with. Rex didn't even know about the hotel – it's not the sort of thing we talked about – but she wouldn't listen when I told her that. So anyhow, I've *told* him since. I mean, why not, when we love each other.'

She paused for breath and Frazer asked, 'Do they know he's here?'

'Of course not! We've gone underground. They weren't even going to let me come fossicking with you because Robert decided he wasn't coming. So now they think I've gone to Surfers' with Jenny Mann and her family. There's going to be a terrific row when they discover I haven't, and you can be sure it'll happen somehow. I always got found out at school, didn't I?'

Always found out and always forgiven. But Frazer wondered if she would be forgiven this time. In her secret heart, she thought Caryl was mistaken about Rex, and she hoped she would fall out of love with him before she did anything silly. Like marrying him.

She said, 'Well, I hope you and Rex have time to help me get that shaft cleared out before you're snatched away, that's all. But they'll have a pretty hard time finding you here.'

'Clear the shaft?' Caryl said. 'What do you mean? I thought you were fooling when you asked Rex if he could use a pick. I thought we just wandered round picking stones up.'

'Not here you don't. Though you just might pick something up if you were dead lucky. I'm afraid it's hard work here. But never mind, Caryl, Rex won't have to be slaving away all the time. And by the way,' she couldn't prevent herself from adding, 'don't you think you should really find out a bit more about him before you—' She stopped and bit her lip.

Caryl said outright, 'Before I jump into bed with him? Don't fret, Fraze, I can look after myself.' With this somewhat cryptic remark she drank down the rest of her tea and then disappeared in the direction of the river to wash.

Frazer mixed the eggs, put them in the pan, and shouted for Rex to wake up. She didn't have any illusions about Rex. She thought he was a drifter and she didn't like his eyes. He reminded her of someone, but she couldn't think who. She suspected too that Caryl's obvious affluence must be at least part of the reason why he was in love with her. She was pretty and bright as well,

43

so he was really on to a good thing. 'Falling in love is a nuisance,' Frazer thought. People were always falling in love with the wrong person, or their relatives thought they were, anyhow . . .

She told Rex caustically when he appeared, his long hair tousled, and stretching his arms above his head, 'You'll have to get up earlier than this other days. Early morning's the best time for heavy work.'

Rex stopped in the middle of a yawn and stared at her. 'Heavy work? I thought we just picked over the stones in some old shaft.'

'Did you? Well, we've got to shift a ton or so of mullock before we even begin,' Frazer said. 'You told me you could use a pick. I suppose you can use a shovel too.'

'Yes, I can use a shovel – if I want to. I thought this was supposed to be a holiday. Now it looks like it's a labour camp instead – with me as the key man. Is that why Caryl asked me along?'

'You'd know better than I,' said Frazer. 'As far as I'm concerned, you're here to provide the brawn.' She began to stir the eggs, her back to him.

He came up behind her and spoke close to her cheek. 'And you'll provide the brains, will you? And the beauty.' He put his arms suddenly and exploringly around her. Frazer dropped the spoon and pulled away.

'Leave me alone!' she said sharply, the colour bright in her face.

He looked at her thoughtfully. 'You intrigue me, Frazer. I haven't sized you up yet. It should be an interesting exercise.'

'Then do it all in your head,' snapped Frazer, and added, 'I wish you hadn't come.'

'Oh, come on now – you've just admitted you need my muscles. What have I done that you don't like me?'

'Nothing – yet.'

'But I'd better watch it, had I?'

'Yes.'

'That goes for you too, or you might find yourself all on your own. *Then* what?'

44

'Then I'd be on my own, that's all.'

'You'd stay here?' His light grey eyes were curious and intent.

'Yes. I've come here with a purpose – even if you haven't.'

'Oh, I've got a purpose all right, don't worry.'

'But it hasn't anything to do with opals, has it?' she challenged, thinking of Caryl, pretty, and rich—

Rex didn't answer, because Caryl came back then. Instead, he kissed her, and said over her head, 'It's a pity you haven't a boy-friend too, Fraze,' and went off to have his wash.

CHAPTER THREE

Iᴛ hadn't been a good start to the day, but Frazer forgot it all later when they started to clear the shaft.

For some reason Rex appeared to have decided to put in a morning of good hard work. He listened agreeably while Frazer explained what had to be done, added a few suggestions of his own, and was soon at work with the pick loosening up the mullock, while Frazer manipulated the shovel and bucket to clear the loosened rock and dirt from the shaft.

Caryl, wearing enormous pink sunglasses, took a turn with the shovel, but prove herself so inept she retired to the sidelines, and contented herself with watching and making an occasional amusing or encouraging remark. At lunch time, she was the one who made the sandwiches from the bread and tomatoes and cheese that Frazer had bought in Minning Minning, and prepared mugs of instant coffee. Frazer ate her share quickly, then went to walk slowly up the slope, looking for signs of exposed opal dirt that might tell her roughly how deep the shaft was likely to be and thus how much rubbish they had yet to clear out of it.

Rex joined her after a few minutes, a sandwich in his hand.

'What are you looking for, Frazer?'

'I'm interested to work out how deep that shaft's likely to be.'

He looked at her sceptically. 'How do you reckon you're going to do that?'

'If you're interested I'll tell you,' said Frazer, who had stooped to examine the dirt under some low brush.

'I'm interested, don't worry.'

On the principle that it didn't hurt anyone to know a little about what they were doing, she explained to him briefly that opals were found in the dirt that underlay the

46

desert sandstone and its so-called iron band. When a man sank a shaft, he had to get through the sandstone topping before he could begin tunnelling.

'So you see, if I can find where the opal dirt begins on this slope, we'll have an idea just how deep the shaft's likely to be, and how much mullock we're likely to have to shovel out, since some idiot decided to put it back in the mine.'

'Some idiot? You mean Dexter?'

For some obscure reason, Frazer said, 'How would I know? It might have been other fossickers.' In her heart she knew it must have been Dexter, but it was knowledge she wasn't going to share with Rex.

'You're quite a character, aren't you?' he said. He had stuffed the rest of the sandwich into his mouth, and with a stout stick he had found he began scratching about in the dirt where they had stopped. 'I don't think I've ever met anyone quite like you, and I've been around. Where did you get all your info, by the way? It wasn't from Geology lessons at school, I'll bet.'

Frazer shrugged. 'Oh, I've fossicked for opals before this.'

'Ever find anything?'

'Yes.'

'Worth much?'

'Don't you know anything?' Frazer exclaimed. 'Aren't you even in the least interested in opals? What did you come for?'

'Various reasons. Because Caryl asked me in the first place,' he said offhandedly. 'But I could get very interested.'

'It might be worth your while,' said Frazer. 'There are opals here all right, and if we're lucky we could make a lot of money. I suppose money interests you?'

'Sure, money interests me — I just don't like to have to work too hard to get it, that's all. So I'd like to know why you're so certain there's something here before I kill myself shovelling dirt. Come on now — where did you get your steer?'

'I'm not going to tell you,' said Frazer flatly, and added cryptically, 'Don't forget I work on my uncle's newspaper. Or didn't Caryl tell you that?'

She thought he looked a little bit impressed, but he merely said, 'No, she didn't,' and Frazer stooped to examine the dirt he had been scratching at. It was red and it was sandstone, and they both moved a little lower down the slope. A little later they found some very hard rock and Frazer was certain it was the ironstone band that capped the opal dirt, and she felt sure now that the shaft wasn't going to be all that deep.

'Once we've got that mullock out of the way, we can really start getting excited,' she said jubilantly.

'You really believe in it, don't you?' Rex commented. They were heading back to the camp and Caryl. 'I think I'm going to stick to you, Frazer. As the key man, I'll be entitled to a full share of anything we turn up. What we find's going to be ours, isn't it? The brawn's entitled to as much as the brain when the brain can't manage alone.'

'Yes,' said Frazer after a moment. She hadn't thought ahead in that particular direction, and she spoke reluctantly because the way she saw it, if they found the Shining Flame, the Palace of Fire, the Princess – then it would be her father's. Not to be sold for money. To be loved and admired and dreamed over. Still, there would be other opals. She just wished she didn't feel this way about Rex, because of course you shared with the mates who worked with you. Caryl, she knew, didn't care one way or the other. Rex was what interested her most. Frazer wished vainly that she could have been working with someone who understood and who shared her dedication, but the only person she could think of like that was her father. Unexpectedly, she found herself thinking of Jay Dexter, but before she set off on a train of thought that involved having him working with her, she switched her mind to something else. She didn't want to think about Jay Dexter.

She was thankful when Rex said, 'I remember seeing a film on TV once about opal mining – people living under the ground in houses they'd dug out. They had furniture, refrigerators – television – the lot.'

'Coober Pedy,' said Frazer. 'It means white man in a hole. The aboriginals gave it that name when they saw the miners there.'

'Have you been there?' Rex asked curiously.

'No, we never—' She stopped and started again. She wasn't going to talk to Rex about her father, about her childhood. 'It's in South Australia.'

Caryl came over from the camp to meet them, and she hooked her arm rather possessively through Rex's and asked, 'What have you two been talking about?'

It seemed a curious question to ask, or perhaps it was the way Caryl asked it. Rex answered before Frazer could speak.

'Frazer's been telling me all about opals. Seems to me we might as well stay awhile and give it a go, Caryl. I might finish up a millionaire. I'd even be able to buy a motorbike,' he added cynically.

'But you have a motorbike,' said Frazer, frowning. She was eager to get back to the shaft, but she didn't like to push the others too hard.

'Oh no, I haven't,' said Rex. 'It's Caryl's.'

'It's *ours*,' said Caryl, then amended it. 'At least, it's yours. It's no use to me – I can't ride it and my parents would never let me learn.'

'You could learn out here. I'll teach you if we stay.'

Caryl brightened up. 'That would be super. When can we start? Now?'

'Some other time,' said Rex. 'Right now we're going to get some more of that mullock shifted.'

Caryl looked a little downcast, but she didn't protest. She was meeker than she had been at school, Frazer thought, but perhaps that was what love did to you. She put on her sunglasses and her cotton hat and trailed along behind Rex.

This time Frazer took her tape recorder with her. She thought it might entertain Caryl. She had bought several tapes while she was in Sydney – Beethoven, Mozart,

Chopin, Liszt – things she could listen to for ever.

'There's no doubt about you girls,' Rex commented after she had set it going and gone to join him. He was swinging the pick and breaking up the heavy mullock, and Frazer picked up the shovel and set to work too. 'You do things in style, don't you? I can't say I'm crazy about working to that sort of music, not that I'm a peasant, but I'd choose something lighter. Your folks must be pretty good to you, anyhow. What business are they in?'

'I don't have folks,' said Frazer briefly. 'Only an uncle and aunt, and my uncle runs a newspaper.'

'Must be money in it. That school you and Caryl went to cost plenty, I'll bet. Or did your father leave you a mint?'

Caryl was sitting with the tape recorder several yards up the slope, in the shade of some stunted trees, and Frazer didn't like the considering way Rex was looking at her. She didn't think Caryl would have liked it either. She said chillingly, 'You ask a lot of questions, don't you? Are you going to tell me what business your father's in and where you went to school? I don't really want to know, anyway, I'd much rather you got on with the work.'

'Right,' he said. 'We'll leave each other's pasts alone. I haven't got anything to hide, by the way, but I'm beginning to suspect you have – unless you just like being mysterious.'

Frazer didn't rise to that bait, and they went on working in silence. The sun was hot and Frazer was perspiring. Rex had taken off his shirt and revealed a torso that was surprisingly sinewy, and Frazer asked on impulse, 'What do you do when you're not on vacation, Rex?'

'Vacation? You must be joking. I've never worked so hard. You're not supposed to ask questions, but I'll answer you. I've worked on the roads – delivered milk – sold burglar alarms and encyclopaedias— Well, you name it, I've done it. Everything except dig for opals – and of course the other things that parents of nice girls always want the men who fall for their daughters to do. Next time I'll pick a girl without a father, I think.' He grinned and looked up, and Frazer discovered that Caryl had strolled over.

'Fool!' said Caryl, smiling back at him. But she looked a shade uncertain.

Frazer went on shovelling the mullock. If she'd been Caryl she wouldn't have liked that remark. But then she didn't understand men – not in personal relationships.

Her muscles were aching when at last they tossed it in and went wearily back to the camp. They all walked in silence, and glancing across the plain in the direction of the homestead, Frazer caught a flash of light and then another one. Rex, who had followed her gaze, said dryly, 'Someone's watching us through binoculars. Guess who?' He flung an arm in a comradely way across Frazer's shoulders as he spoke, and she moved sharply away from him.

Caryl said, 'Wouldn't you love a nice steak for dinner, Rex? And some crisp and crunchy fresh bread rolls? Why don't we go and eat in Minning Minning? The thought of – well, what're we having tonight, Frazer? Whatever it is, I just know it won't appeal to me.'

'Tinned tuna and tomatoes and onions,' said Frazer. She had done most of the cooking for herself and her father, and that had been one of their favourite dishes – with lots of pepper and sometimes an egg or two mixed in. And a thick slice of bread to wipe up the plate.

Caryl didn't comment. She said, 'Why don't we go up to the homestead and see if we can get some steak there? After all, this is a cattle station. They must have loads of steak waiting to be eaten.'

Frazer shook her head. 'It wouldn't be any use.'

'Want to bet?' Caryl's green eyes were alight with mischief and Frazer remembered what she had said that morning – about charming Jay Dexter.

'No,' said Frazer. 'We're just not going.'

'Rex,' said Caryl, 'you'd like steak, wouldn't you?

'My very oath I would.'

Frazer said 'No' again, but all the same, before she had even had a chance to clean herself up, she and Caryl were on one of the bikes careering across the paddock. Rex had egged Caryl on and it had been two against one. If Frazer hadn't gone, then Rex would have, and as he had said himself, 'A couple of pretty girls have more pull than a bum like me, so don't be hard to get on with, Frazer.'

Caryl hadn't enjoyed the day much. Frazer was aware of this though nothing had been said. She had seen next to nothing of Rex, and she had probably been bored. Now she wanted a bit of excitement, she wanted to work up some kind of escapade. She had been like that at school. Boredom, monotony, had been her enemies. As they rode along the track Frazer called back over her shoulder, 'It won't be so dull once we've cleared out that shaft. We can really start looking for opals then.'

'Oh – opals,' Caryl said dismissively, and Frazer felt dashed.

The sun hadn't yet set when they reached the garden that surrounded the homestead. Frazer thought hopefully that perhaps Dexter would not yet be back from working on the run – though if that had been him watching them through fieldglasses then he was home. She hoped they would see not him, but his sister Barbara, anyhow. Because she didn't want to ask favours of him, and no matter what Caryl thought, she was sure her experience didn't qualify her to dazzle a man like Jay Dexter.

They dismounted from the bike and went through the garden. No lights shone from the house yet, but perhaps it was too early. They climbed the steps and knocked at the wire screen door. While they waited, Caryl looked back across the garden and remarked, 'It's quite a nice garden. Doesn't look a palatially big homestead, though. Do you know if he's married?'

She spoke softly, but Frazer felt uneasy. She would hate Jay Dexter to hear them talking about him. She kept her voice even lower as she said, 'No, he's not.'

'He can't be that bad-tempered, surely,' Caryl said with a giggle. 'And he is handsome. I think I like older men – there's something exciting about them. They know things – they must.'

Frazer didn't comment. She was quite sure Jay Dexter

knew plenty – far more than she or Caryl would ever know between them ... No one came to the door, not even when Caryl knocked again and called out loudly, 'Is anyone at home?'

Frazer drew a deep breath of relief, though, curiously, she felt let down too. She told Caryl, 'There's no one about. We might as well forget it.'

Frazer drew a deep breath of relief, though, curiously, she felt let down too. She told Caryl, 'There's no one about. We might as well forget it.'

They both went down the steps, Caryl saying petulantly, 'I hate being thwarted. I want that steak – I practically promised Rex we'd get it. Why don't we go to the back and see if the cook's about? There must be someone – he can't live all by himself—' She stopped speaking abruptly, and Frazer saw what she had seen at exactly that instant.

Jay Dexter coming through the oleander trees and across the lawn towards them.

They both stayed where they were, though Frazer had a childish impulse to run away, as if she had been caught trespassing. He didn't wear a hat, and his forehead was smudged with red dust. The forest green shirt he wore with the sleeves rolled up made his skin – his face, his arms and his neck – look more deeply tanned than ever, while the light-coloured narrow-legged drill trousers and tan boots accentuated his height. He wasn't half as dirty as Frazer felt, but he would soon be on his way to the shower, that was for sure. He stopped dead in his tracks a few paces away and looked at them impatiently.

'What's the matter now? What do you two girls want here?'

Frazer felt rather than saw Caryl stiffen, and there was a moment's silence. Frazer rather meanly said nothing, because after all it hadn't been her idea to come here. *She* wasn't the one who wanted the steak. Then Caryl rallied, and in a voice that was soft and wooing said, 'We're *hungry*, Mr. Dexter. We'd like some steak.' She moved forward until she stood no more than a foot away from

Jay Dexter and she looked up at him. Caryl was small, and Frazer could just imagine those green eyes of hers looking at him appealingly.

While he stood silent, saying nothing at all.

Caryl chattered on. 'We knocked at the door, and no one came. Do you live here all alone, Mr. Dexter? Oh, how I envy you! Do you know, we haven't even a bath? Imagine it – no lovely tub to wallow in after a hard day's work.'

Frazer closed her eyes for a second, squirming inwardly. Oh, she would eat dirt rather than talk to that man the way Caryl was doing! And it was having not the slightest effect on him.

He looked over Caryl's head at Frazer. 'Too bad,' he drawled. 'So whose idea was it that you should come here roughing it? Don't blame me. Did I ask you to come and set up your pitiful camp on my property? It's your own idea entirely. Believe me, I've other things to do with my time than play nursemaid to a bunch of no-hopers. If you don't like it, then you know what to do.'

Frazer was not in the least surprised to hear him saying these things, but she heard Caryl's gasp of indignation and knew that she was.

'No-hopers! We're – we're as respectable as you are! We're looking for opals – it's all perfectly legitimate,' she exclaimed, outraged.

Frazer saw him smile slightly. 'Okay, it's legitimate, but I don't have to like it, do I? And you can get it right out of that red head of yours that I'm susceptible to the charms of schoolgirls. I'm not. Moreover, it's not going to keep me awake at night that you can't eat steak or take a bath. In fact, I just don't want to know. Good evening.'

Before either of them was aware of it, he had brushed by them, mounted the steps, and gone inside, letting the wire door slam behind him.

Caryl was furious. 'What a vile man! Oh, I've never been treated like that in my life! As though we were riffraff! He's – he's inhuman!'

Privately Frazer agreed. She had known long before

she had ever met him that Jay Dexter was inhuman and he was certainly living up to her expectations. She didn't remind Caryl that *she* hadn't wanted to come here begging favours from him, she merely agreed that he was hateful and that it was plain if they wanted steak they would have to get it elsewhere.

'Well, I do want steak,' said Caryl. 'And I'm not going to sit down outside a tent eating tinned fish while he lords it up here and looks at us through binoculars and gloats. We'll go to Minning Minning – we've got plenty of money. We could stay the night at the motel. You and Rex need a soak in a hot bath – you'll be stiff as boards tomorrow.'

It was a temptation and Frazer almost gave in to it. She thought it over while they tootled back to the camp in the deepening darkness. She thought more of the bath than she did of the steak, which she could easily forgo. Obviously she couldn't take a dip in the creek tonight. Apart from the fact that it was dark, it would be too cold now. Otherwise there was just the plastic basin she had bought in Minning. She could heat some water and have a good wash in her tent, but a wash was not a good hot soak. Yet to go to Minning seemed a sign of weakness. She wouldn't put it past Jay Dexter to come checking up at dawn tomorrow, and she wanted to be on deck, working and full of vitality. To prove that she didn't depend on him – that she had chosen this life and she could take it. To prove that *she* didn't need his steak or the use of his bathtub. She had done without most of the luxuries of life for her first fourteen years, and she didn't need the soft things now. Her father had roughed it here, and so would she.

By the time they got back to the camp, she had quite made up her mind. She listened to Caryl's recital of Jay Dexter's insufferable inhospitality—

'And I thought country people were supposed to be so friendly! Well, all the ones I've met socially *are*. But you'd have thought Frazer and I were a couple of tramps. I'd just like to tell him what school I went to and who my father is, and—'

'Oh, quit belly-aching, Caryl,' Rex interrupted. 'You can't expect everyone to fall for your charms. Let's forget it all and get in to Minning and buy ourselves a feed or whatever you want to do.'

'We'll stay the night,' said Caryl. 'At least then he'll be aware we're not tramps.'

'Who cares what he thinks?' Rex said. 'Okay with you, Frazer?'

Frazer, who hadn't taken part in the conversation, shook her head. 'I'm tired. I'm staying here. You two do what you like.'

Minutes later she watched them go off on the motorbike, and then she lit the lamp, gathered some twigs and bits of wood and lit a small fire in a fireplace they had built with stones. She put some water on to boil and she thought, 'If he looks out now, he'll see that someone doesn't care whether he's hospitable or not.'

She washed in her tent, and got into clean clothes, topping them with a dark track suit. Considerably cleaner, but weary and more than a little stiff, she made herself a tomato omelette and ate a couple of bananas, sitting alone under the trees with the glowing ashes of the fire. She could hear a few night noises – a mopoke owl calling eerily, and far away the distant drumming of an emu. Both were familiar nostalgic sounds, sounds she had often heard at night in the past as she sat with her father over tea or helped him sort the stones he had found that day. Uncle Frank had been right in a way when he had said she couldn't bring back the past. Nothing was really as she had imagined it. Only sounds like this . . .

She felt more than a little sad all on her own, and there was no comfort to be gained from the yellow light away over at the homestead. What was Jay Dexter doing right now? she wondered. Was he alone? Had his sister gone out? Had he too heard the drumming of the emu across the plains, the wailing hoot of the mopoke? Or wasn't he interested in things like that?

Presently she washed her dishes and went into her tent. She put a Mozart tape on the cassette, undressed and got

56

into her sleeping bag, and lay in the dark listening to the music. She wondered if Rex and Caryl would come back tonight or if they would stay in Minning, and she hoped they would return for two reasons. One reason was because Caryl had just left school and she didn't trust Rex. The second was a purely selfish reason. She wanted Rex there to help her in the morning.

Before the tape had clicked off, she was exhaustedly asleep.

She had her wish. Caryl and Rex came back that night, and for the next few days they worked steadily despite aching muscles. Or she and Rex worked. Jay Dexter always turned up at some time or another during the day. He looked over the shaft and he looked over the camp, and he never had much to say. Nor did he ever find anything to complain of.

Caryl said crossly, 'You'd think he'd at least ask if we wanted anything, now he knows we're so well behaved. Why doesn't he?'

'Because he doesn't like us,' said Rex. 'Not even you. And if you will mix with types like me, what can you expect?'

Caryl put her head on one side. She didn't know if he was joking or not. 'Then why don't you shave off your beard and cut your hair?' she said. 'Wouldn't it be worth it if it earned us some steak?'

'You're complaining now, are you?' Rex said mockingly. 'I thought you liked me just as I am. *Frazer* does.'

Frazer said nothing. She knew Caryl was getting restless, was tired of the discomforts and inconvenience of the outdoor camping life and she felt guilty about it. And she didn't at all like the habit Rex had of playing her off against Caryl. It would have been a much more comfortable arrangement in every way if Robert had come as they had planned. As it was, Caryl could think of nothing but Rex, and he, unfortunately for her, had chosen to throw himself more or less wholeheartedly into helping Frazer.

More than once Caryl remarked pointedly that they were wasting their time, that Jay Dexter had said there was nothing to be found at Wandalilli.

'Oh, shut up, Caryl,' said Rex as they sat in the tree shade one lunchtime and she reiterated her opinion. 'You're just a pretty butterfly. Frazer's the one with the clues.'

'Don't fool yourself,' said Caryl, stung. 'She only did Geology at school the same as me.' She picked disconsolately at the salad she had made of what was left of a lettuce, some tomatoes, a tin of pineapple and some sardines.

'She's had some practical experience too,' said Rex. 'You can't beat that. In fact, I'm beginning to think she must have been brought up in the business.' He buttered a slice of stale bread and looked at Frazer speculatively. 'How's that for a guess, Frazer? I'm all for you these days, you know, even if I did think you were some kind of a nut at first.'

The two girls were silent. Caryl didn't look at all pleased, and Frazer always felt ill at ease when Rex said things like that. She was quite certain he was 'all for her' simply because he hoped there might be money in it for him, but Caryl probably thought he meant something quite different. And even if she suspected he was teasing, it was teasing that was hurtful and in very poor taste.

Frazer got up from her stool and went to pour the mugs of tea, and when she turned round again she remarked that it was time to get fresh supplies from Minning Minning.

'Right,' said Rex. 'Let's call a halt to the day's work and go in this afternoon. You can clean up the dishes, Caryl. Frazer and I'll have to change into something that won't make you ashamed of us – we're the dirty ones.'

Caryl said nothing. She kept her eyes lowered and she stayed where she was, and Frazer saw her mouth tremble slightly. She said, 'I'll do the dishes, Caryl. I don't want to go into town, as a matter of fact.'

'Of course you do.' Rex, about to head into his tent,

looked back. 'You've been working just as hard as me – you need a break, a bit of relaxation. We'll all go into the pub and eat and have a few drinks and find somewhere to dance. Come on now, Fraze – get moving, make yourself pretty.'

Frazer shook her head. She had no intention of going in with them – and certainly not if they were dancing. Heaven knew what kind of trouble Rex would stir up then! She didn't want to be on bad terms with Caryl simply because of his callousness. She said, 'My muscles rebel at the idea of riding all that way. I'd far sooner relax here at the camp.'

Rex frowned. 'I don't like the sound of that – I've got a suspicious mind. If you stay here, you better lie doggo in your tent and pretend to be away. The squatter hasn't been around today so far. Promise now – or I shan't go.'

To her annoyance, Frazer felt herself redden. She had forgotten Jay Dexter hadn't been around yet – and it very nearly made her change her mind and go with the others. Very nearly, but not quite. Because why should she run away? Dexter would come, he would look about, he would find everything in order and he would go. And Frazer just possibly might say sarcastically, 'I'm so sorry we've disappointed you again.'

When the others left, she called out warningly, 'Don't forget to close the gate!'

She watched the motorbike go bumping along, following the line of trees that edged the river, and then when she could no longer hear it or see it, she drew a deep breath, aware of a sense of release. Her first thought was to fly up the hillside to the shaft – her shaft, her father's shaft; to stand there all alone and dream of what was hidden down there waiting for her to find it – to bring it to the sunlight where it could show its secret fires. And then she forced herself to sober down, to be sensible. She must wash the dishes first – she didn't want Jay Dexter to come and see litter about, to say they were living like gypsies.

So she did the dishes, and she tidied up around the tents. Then she combed her tawny hair and clipped it back with the little silver hair ornament her father had bought her once to celebrate a find, then walked across the paddock and up the slope to her little world of make-believe. She kicked around on the hillside as she climbed, picking up stones and examining them as her father had taught her to do, hoping all the time to catch the gleam of glass, the glint of fire.

From the shaft she looked across the lands that belonged to Jay Dexter, as she told herself, 'If I lived here – if all this land were mine – I'd be watching out for opal all the time. If I were riding a horse behind the cattle, half my mind would be on the ground and what might lie under it.' She looked at the shovel and she looked at the bucket, and for once she felt too weary to make the effort to work. Soon now – maybe even tomorrow – they would have all that mullock shifted and they would be down there tunnelling. Frazer's mind raced ahead. She imagined her own cry of delight and excitement when they struck their patch of opal. And they would – she knew they would.

As she stood staring down at the ground, like a little streak of lightning the thought flashed through her mind, 'Will we?'

It was the first doubt she had known and it shook her. It was as though her faith had a crack in it. And she blamed it instantly on Jay Dexter, for being so discouraging – for his own purposes. A hard man, she thought, who had never thrilled to the beauty of the opal or marvelled that such fire and light and glory could come whole from the dark earth. What was the earth to him – the red mysterious earth that beckoned and challenged and promised? Her eyes narrowed, she stared across at the homestead, vaguely anticipating his visit to the camp. As she looked, she saw two people – two tiny figures – emerge from the trees around the garden. They went towards the garages, and a couple of minutes later they drove away in a car – the way Rex and Caryl had gone.

So he had gone out! He and his sister must have business to do in Minning. Great! He wouldn't be coming over here to see what was going on . . . Curiously, she felt piqued as well as relieved. It was almost as though she had been waiting for him to come, and yet she hadn't. Now she thought, 'What shall I do?' She felt aimless, even despondent, all of a sudden. She began to walk higher up the hillside in the hot sunshine. She should have gone to Minning Minning – she could still go, if she wanted to. But Minning was a small town – she might run into Jay Dexter there, so she couldn't possibly go, now. She stood quite still, aware of anticlimax; and a warm wind, a wind that smelled of dust and yet was a friendly wind, lifted the hair from her neck with a touch that was almost sensual. She looked out over Jay Dexter's country – a land of dried grasses, of dark patchy scrub and little twisted trees. *This* was his earth – and now her eyes had picked out a cloud of dust over the plain, and there were men on horseback and cattle that they were mustering from the scrub-scribbled paddock. Frazer felt a stirring in her heart and she thought of the grandfather whom she had never met. He was dead now, and he had been ruined by drought – and she had never visited him for a holiday, never learned to ride a horse—

Almost without thinking, she ran down the slope, across the flat, got on her bike and was racing off across the paddock in search of those stockmen and the cattle.

It was further than she had expected. There were two gates to open and close, and then she was put-putting very quietly and steadily over the ground towards the swirling clouds of dust. There were some box trees where she would stop and from whose shelter she could watch and decide whether or not it would be possible to go and talk to some of the stockmen.

She reached the trees and waited, still astride her bike, one foot on the ground. She watched the men as well as the shining beasts they were drawing into a tight and ever-growing mob as they were brought in from the scrub. They all looked so skilled on their horses, so sure, so confident, and they all looked much the same with their broad-brimmed hats, checked shirts, dusty boots and trousers. She had picked out Jay Dexter very easily that first day she came to Wandalilli. She had thought it rather clever of her at the time, but now she knew it hadn't been so clever. The fact was, there was something very distinctive about Jay Dexter that made him stand out from other men. Not one of those stockmen she was watching could possibly be mistaken for Dexter. She didn't know exactly what quality it was that he possessed, but it came across strongly and unmistakably. It was a bit like warming to opal, she thought, staring through the dust at the activity that was going on. Like just *knowing* when you were getting on to opal, as her father had always claimed he knew – even though he had never been lucky enough to strike a really fabulous patch.

It was strange, Frazer reflected, that not one of the men rode over to speak to her or to see what she wanted. Strange and a little unflattering – because they knew she was there. Now if Caryl had been there, it would have been different. Caryl had just a dash of the woman of the world about her. Frazer was still – well, what was she? She wasn't a child, she wasn't a woman. Living on the opal fields, mixing with all sorts of men, had still taught her nothing about the other sex. And now, when every one of those stockmen glanced her way occasionally yet not one of them rode over towards her, she knew she was just not going to have the courage to take the first step. It was strange, because when she had first come to Wandalilli she wouldn't have hesitated. She *hadn't* hesitated – she had approached Jay Dexter himself. Somewhere along the line, she appeared to have lost the innocence of her confidence.

So there was no point in sitting here any longer.

She revved up and was about to roar round in a defiant sweep and head back for the camp when a voice like an arrow shot her in the back.

'Hey, you – Cathleen Dwight – stay where you are!'

Frazer was so taken by surprise she did exactly as she

was told, looking back wide-eyed over her shoulder to see Jay Dexter come thundering towards her on a tall horse. The horse was red and Jay Dexter looked like some satanic prince on its back, so high above her, his hat in his hand, his thick black hair gleaming in the dusty glare of the sunlight. He reined in and swung down from the saddle.

'I thought you understood you were confined to a certain area.'

'I – I came for a ride,' Frazer quavered, and added like an idiot, 'I thought you'd gone to town.'

'My God, what a naïve confession! Or is it to let me know you weren't looking for me? All the same, I wouldn't advise you to try chatting up my stockmen – they might misunderstand and you'd find yourself welcoming a nocturnal visitor to your tent. Or is that what you're hoping for?'

Oh, the mockery of those black eyes! Frazer's cheeks flamed.

'I wanted to look – to see what's going on, that's all.'

He looked at her scathingly. 'Come off it, Kate. You'll be telling me you're looking for something for your newspaper column next, trying to persuade me it's a reporting job you're on, and I know damn well it's not.'

'How do you know? Have you been phoning my uncle behind my back – telling tales on me?'

'I haven't found a tale worth the telling yet – but I've been thinking about it,' he assured her, and she had no idea whether he meant it or not. His grim smile had changed to one of quizzical amusement, however, and he commented, 'You're beginning to look bedraggled, Kate. That youthful bloom's brushing off. The river water's not what you'd call kind, is it, when it comes to washing clothes or hair or bodies. Are you missing your home comforts?'

Her cheeks turned fiery red. She knew very well her hair was not at its best, that even the vigorous brushing she gave it night and morning could vanquish the dust gathered daily from the mine. And she knew that her shirt

63

and jeans were pretty dirty. But she didn't care all that much. She never had as a child, and she didn't care now. When she did get a hot shower – and she'd spend a night in Minning just as soon as it suited her to do so – then she'd have the most marvellous feeling of cleanliness and fragrance and the whole world would shine. She looked forward to re-experiencing that sensation so well remembered from childhood.

Meanwhile, of course *he* wouldn't offer the use of the homestead bathroom!

She said carelessly, 'Home comforts don't loom all that large in my life. But you certainly are doing your best to get rid of us, aren't you – with – with inhospitability and daily inspections—'

He frowned. 'Daily inspections? Is that how you think of it? As for inhospitability, I've never pretended I wanted you to stay. Why should I? You're a responsibility—'

'That's not true,' she denied. 'Anyhow, you can't stop us, we've got miners' rights.'

His wide mouth curved sardonically. 'You set great store by those rights, don't you, Kate? But I could stop you staying here if I wanted, never fear. I wouldn't let a little bit of paper stand in my way if I found you too objectionable.'

'I thought you already did.' She was staring straight into the unfathomable darkness of his eyes, and she could see how thick and dark his lashes were. 'I thought you found everyone who came on your property looking for opals objectionable.'

'You did? Now I wonder why.' He felt in his pocket and began abstractedly to roll a cigarette. 'There haven't been all that many opal seekers here – it's not an area that's been publicised, for obvious reasons. For your information – though maybe this is not news to you, I wouldn't know what facts are hoarded up in that perverse head of yours – there's been no one here for something like three years. But I tell you, the last lot were rough as bags. As you see, they didn't waste energy opening up the shaft, but they opened my gates – and left them open. They also drank themselves stupid and littered their camp with broken bottles and any amount of rubbish. The only thing they didn't do – the female members of the contingent didn't try to seduce me. Would you blame me if I found them objectionable?'

Frazer bristled at his reference to seduction – that was Caryl the other night, but surely he needn't put it like that! She was stung by his tone, and irritated that these other people were the reason for the daily inspections. As if she and Caryl – or even Rex! – were in the least like that! She said coldly and unwillingly, 'No, I wouldn't blame you. But everybody's not like that. I want— *We're* not like that and neither was— What about the man who came here first of all? He worked, he sank a shaft, he was a – a prospector, not—' She stopped and swallowed and went on, 'So did you inspect what *he* was doing every day? Did you try to get rid of *him*?' She pulled herself up abruptly. She was getting too emotional, she was remembering the things her father had said about Dexter, and how little Dexter had cared what happened to him. Her eyes were bright with her hatred and she was spoiling for a fight, but that wouldn't get her anywhere. Because he – Dexter – had said, 'I wouldn't let a little bit of paper stand in my way'. And she believed that implicitly – and she wanted to stay.

He was looking at her reflectively and for a moment he didn't speak, then he said coolly, 'This is where we came in, isn't it? On the edge of a story you wanted to hunt up and build into some sort of sensation for your paper. Well, I'm not talking about the past, Kate. You'll get no stories out of me.' He tossed down the cigarette he had barely begun to smoke and ground it out hard in the dust. 'That's final.'

'Well then' – Frazer tossed back her tawny-streaked hair – 'I'd better not waste my time, had I? And you – you'd better go and see what's happening to your precious stock, hadn't you, Mr. Dexter? One of your prize beasts might slip off into the scrub or something while you're here chatting up a mere human being!' She revved up the motor as she spoke and timed it so the last few words were shouted over her shoulder as she shot off and away.

She went straight back to the camp, and she thought, 'So that's why none of those stockmen came and spoke to me – because he was somewhere about watching and they wouldn't dare. I'll bet he's a horrible man to work for.'

She left the thought there, because somehow she wasn't quite convinced of its fairness.

CHAPTER FOUR

CARYL was much more lively when she and Rex arrived back at the camp just on dark. They had brought back some cans of cold drink and a load of food, and they had both taken a bath at the motel.

'We'd have stayed,' Caryl told Frazer as the two girls unpacked the supplies, and decided to cook eggs and chops for dinner. 'But we decided it wouldn't be fair to you, out here all alone in this deadly, dreary place while we were all civilized at Minning.'

Frazer smiled and murmured her gratitude. But as she laid out the chops on a grid to put over the fire, she herself didn't feel even the slightest longing for Minning and the civilization of its motel. She didn't think Rex had minded coming back all that much either. For her, the glow of the camp fire, the great sky with its large white stars, the shadow-dark trees against their indigo back-drop, held far more magnetism than the pseudo-soph-istication of any little outback town. And when they were sitting around the fire on their campstools, relishing slightly burnt chops, sizzling eggs, and thick slices of fresh, buttered bread, she thought that surely even Caryl must be a little won over.

'I could live this way for ever,' she told herself, and didn't stop to consider whether or not it was quite true.

After they had cleared up their mess, Caryl walked over to Rex and put her arms around his neck, and he drew her to him and kissed her. Frazer knew suddenly that she couldn't sit with them by the fire they had kept going. She would be an unwanted third. She moved away from them casually.

'I'm going for a walk by the river. I'll see you in the morning.'

She took her pocket torch and walked purposefully away over the flat and through the trees that lined the

67

river bank. There was a moon, small and golden, rather than silver, low in the sky, and the night was warmer than usual – a lovely night for a moonlit walk. Frazer slipped through the tree shadows, flickering her torch about. She had never been afraid of the dark, and the soft night sounds were familiar from her childhood. She felt mentally tired and was determined – though futilely – not to do any thinking. The fact was, this business was not turning out the way she had imagined it, and she was not altogether sure what had gone wrong. She couldn't blame it all on Rex's having come instead of Robert, but there seemed to be a vast unbridgeable gap between the dream and the reality, and deep down, she was a little frightened by the thought of her own future. She had pictured it for so long as a continuation of her childhood with her father. Now she knew it was not going to be that, could not possibly be, and an abyss already yawned in front of her before she was ready to look ahead.

She didn't know how long or how far she had been walking when she was startled out of deep abstraction by the sound of other footsteps crunching over the dry gum leaves. The beam of a torch reached blindly and briefly for her eyes, then swooped down to the ground again, and Jay Dexter's voice said, 'So it's you again, Kate.'

Frazer stopped walking. She heard her own breath on an exaggerated and exasperated sigh. 'Aren't I allowed to walk around here, either? You'll have to build a stockade for me, Mr. Dexter. Though I'm not really doing any harm – I'm not smashing up any bottles and I haven't opened a single gate.'

There was silence for a moment. The small pool of light stayed steady at his feet, and suddenly she flicked her own torch upwards and directed it at his face. His dark brows were drawn, and then his eyes were glittering at her and his lips had twisted into an ironic smile. Somehow disconcerted, she let the beam fall and switched off the torch, hardly realizing that he had begun to move towards her.

'The men's quarters are nearby,' he remarked conversationally.

'So what?' said Frazer. 'I'm not afraid of the men.'

'Then you damn well should be,' he snapped. 'They've seen you around — they know you've got good looks. What's more, you might guess the idea they have of you — the three of you — shacking up together under the trees. I'll guarantee it's occurred to more than one of them that the odd girl out will be getting hungry.'

'Hungry?' Frazer repeated, shaken. 'I don't know what you mean. Hungry for — for what?'

'For this,' he bit out. He moved quickly, snapped off his torch and then her arms were pinioned against her sides, and his mouth was against hers in a kiss that frightened her by the violence of its impact, despite the fact that it lasted only a second.

Freed, she thrust her knuckles hard against her lips and gasped out the first words that came. 'Oh — you haven't shaved—'

She heard his incredulous laugh. 'If you're so choosy I'm the more astounded at you for hanging about.' Then with a swift change of tone, he gripped her arm hard, swung her about and began marching her back through the trees. 'Get moving, Kate. I've had enough of this. Get back where you belong and quit making a damn nuisance of yourself!'

She stumbled along in silence till they reached the camp and the dying fire. From one of the tents sounded soft voices and stifled laughter, so that Jay Dexter as well as herself knew that Caryl and Rex were in there making love — or fooling about.

'You'd better get to bed too,' he said tersely, and in a moment she was alone, standing motionless, her mind a ripple with vague troubled waves. She hadn't bargained on this sort of complication when she had made her plans to come to Wandalilli. She had thought about opals and her father's dream, and the reflected shine of the past. Not about being tied up with Caryl and her love affairs. Not, her thoughts continued relentlessly as she forced herself to move into the warm darkness of her own small tent, not of being kissed by *Jay Dexter*. Her fingers went briefly to the soft warmth of her lips. A kiss that was not a kiss. Not in the least a kiss – though it was the first time any man had kissed her since Dave had tried years ago when she was fourteen. A kiss that was intended as a warning against the hot desires of men – as though she needed that warning . . .

He came to the camp again late the following day. She and Rex had worked hard, the pile of mullock was nearly defeated, and now Caryl had persuaded Rex to take her out on the bike – give her a lesson.

Jay Dexter cantered up on his horse, reined in and looked down at Frazer as she set the fire in the fireplace they had improvised. His dark eyes were expressionless, but there was a mocking curve on his wide mouth.

'Is there anything you want?' he asked without more than a nod of greeting.

For an instant the words didn't even make sense to Frazer, so deeply was she embarrassed by the memory of their encounter last night. Yet there was not even the fleeting shadow of shared memory lying within the dark eyes that gazed down at her.

'Nothing,' she said then, and she could hear the resentment and hatred in her own voice.

She thought he hesitated, and then with a slight lift of his dark brows he turned his horse's head and moved away across grasses that were colourless in the fading daylight and would soon flare fiery red as the sun neared the horizon. Frazer watched him go and wondered about him. He was a person, not just a name. Jay Dexter. She stood motionless, a bundle of dry tangy eucalyptus twigs in her hand. Had it been he or had it been his father who had rejected Lee Madigan – who must have his death on his conscience? The thought came from nowhere, and crazily she wanted to run after him and ask. But the tall red horse had broken into a canter, and she stayed where she was and knew that she couldn't have asked anyhow. And she wasn't ready yet to tell him she was Lee Madigan's daughter. There rose in her mind as she stood there the picture of her father as she knew him best: dusty and shabby in his working clothes, his dreaming blue eyes, his kind but obstinate mouth. She remembered the poetry he used to recite for her benefit – long passages from Shakespeare, from Tennyson, even the occasional Australian bush ballad; and the records he had played on the battered old gramophone, classics that gave her a musical appreciation very early in life. He had been an opal miner, and he was rough in many ways and they had led, she supposed, looking back, a strange life together. Yet he was well educated too, and she had a sudden baffling awareness that she had known next to nothing about him. She had no notion why he had chosen to live as he did when he had a wife and a girl-child to care for. Was it an obstinate defiance of the parents of the girl he had married? Or had opals meant more to him than people – more than wife or child?

Suddenly Frazer didn't like her thoughts.

'The happiest time of my life was when I was with Dad,' she reminded herself sombrely. She stooped to the fireplace and carefully arranged her sticks and leaves. She took matches from the pocket of her jeans and in a few seconds her nostrils were filled with the nostalgic scent of burning gum leaves.

Two more days of hard work and the shaft was practically clear. Caryl played cook and had begun fossicking around on the slope and life was proceeding more smoothly. She told Rex gaily, 'I was always tiny. I'll find myself a lump of opal as big as your head while you and Frazer are digging and sweating and shovelling down in that hole.'

Frazer, although there was no hope of that, encouraged her to look. 'You might pick up enough potch and colour to make a pair of ear-rings or even a bracelet. I could face the stones for you.'

The third day, Caryl tired of it. She had had more than enough, and she had found exactly nothing. She hung around the shaft watching and commenting and trying so hard to tempt Rex away that Frazer felt embarrassed when he wouldn't be diverted. At last she drifted off and Frazer and Rex worked on in silence. They had discovered there were two drives opening off the shaft, and Frazer could see that one of them was pretty long. Her heart felt sore as she thought of all the work her father must have put in alone, and she knew that he couldn't have found what he sought there or he wouldn't have opened another drive.

Rex, sweating over shovelling out the clayey opal dirt that blocked off the second drive, asked without turning his head, 'What's the idea of these tunnels, Frazer? Shouldn't we be sifting through all this muck we're tossing out?'

Frazer filled a bucket with loosened mullock as she answered, 'We could, but I don't think we need bother.' Her father, she was sure, would have gone through it pretty thoroughly. She went on to answer his first question, wiping her forehead with a dirty hand. 'You tunnel so you can look for opal in the roof – that's the ironstone band that separates the sandstone from the opal dirt. You could find a seam of opal there, if you were lucky – like a sheet of mosaic, all in pieces, each piece an opal, maybe cardboard-thin, maybe an inch thick.'

Rex grunted and paused for a moment, his light grey eyes looking at her hard. 'Worth what?' he asked briefly.

Frazer shrugged. 'It depends on a lot of things – on weight and colour and pattern and so on. It wouldn't be too much to expect to find a few stones worth a thousand or so dollars each, with prices what they are these days.'

Rex whistled softly. 'So that's why we're working so feverishly! Let's get on with it!' And as he turned away again he added, 'You're an enigma, Frazer. One of these days I'd like to hear the story of your life.'

Frazer felt something in her tighten and close up. Rex would never hear the story of her life. Never. He wasn't her sort of person. She had thought once that she would like to marry a man who was as fiercely wrapped up in opal mining as she was. But it wouldn't be anyone like Rex who didn't know what it was to thrill to the sheer beauty of the opal. She remembered poignantly how reluctant her father had always been to sell the best stones he found. He was a good man, she thought, warm and loving, and the thought somehow relieved her because lately her idea of him seemed to have becoming wavering and uncertain as though she no longer trusted the vision of a child.

Ten minutes later Caryl reappeared, wearing a cheap ankle-length cotton dress she had bought once in Minning – for a joke. It was orange and pink and though it clashed hideously with her red hair she looked like some colourful and fantastic dancer in it. She began to sway about at the top of the shaft, singing some pop song in her slightly flat husky voice, and quite suddenly Rex tossed down his shovel, leapt out of the hole in the ground and began to chase her over the slope.

Frazer, weary and hot, climbed out too and watched them smiling. Then Rex caught Caryl and they rolled over and over on the ground till they fetched up against a scrubby bush, their bodies interlocked, and began kissing. Frazer looked away, uneasy. Jay Dexter hadn't been to check up on them for a couple of days, and now would be just the time he would turn up. To her relief he was nowhere to be seen and she thanked heaven for it – a little prematurely, as she was to discover later.

When the other two quit fooling about, they went over to the camp. 'Come and have a pre-luncheon drink, Frazer,' Caryl said as they went. 'I've got some cans of beer cooling down in the waterhole.'

'I'll be over later,' Frazer said. She didn't like beer, and just now she didn't feel like joining the others. She went down into the mine again, as though it were some kind of escape. Her mind was in a strange sort of turmoil. Seeing Caryl and Rex kissing like that had brought back with a sharp astringency the memory of Jay Dexter and the brief meaningless pressure of his lips on hers in the warm darkness by the river. 'My one and only kiss,' she thought.

'While Rex is always and openly kissing Caryl.' And what did those kisses mean – to Rex, to Caryl? More, she suspected, to Caryl than they did to Rex. Suddenly she wished achingly that she were older and knew more about love and life – she who had always been so confident about her worldly experience.

The day had become ominously hot and the sun had a harsh coppery tinge about it. She had noticed great clouds swarming low on the far horizon when she had been watching Rex chase Caryl. Restless, she clambered over the last small heap of mullock and peered into the second drive her father had made. She could see the careful, almost regular pick marks he had made. He hadn't driven far under the sandstone here because – Frazer caught her lips between her teeth remembering – because he had been ill, and he had never come back. But he had hoped – he had believed – as he had chipped away, cramped, at the roof of the tunnel, that the find of his life – the Wandalilli Princess – was almost in his hands.

Preoccupied with her thoughts, Frazer scarcely knew she had reached behind her for the small pick, and now she was gouging carefully with the chisel point into the earth just under the roof. She wasn't sure where her thoughts had led her by the time, but subconsciously she was listening for the sound that would mean the pick had struck a hard seam of opal. She was dirty, and she was hot and perspiring and more than a little tired when something made her stop chipping and look across her shoulder to the top of the shaft.

Jay Dexter stood there, a shadow against the hot haziness of the sky, and she felt her heart lurch.

He looked down at her, his broad-brimmed hat tipped back on his head, a thick lock of dark hair making a splotch of shadow against the tan of his brow. He finished rolling a cigarette, stuck down the paper, and as he struck a match tossed down at her dryly, casually, 'You have a woman's disregard of logic, Kate.'

Frazer felt herself contract into hostility. Wouldn't it have been a change if he had made some kindly inquiry

74

instead? 'How you going, mate?' That's what they had always asked on the opal fields when she had worked with her father. But Jay Dexter had to say she had a woman's disregard of logic!

And who had ever asked him to call her Kate? she wondered as she stared up at him blankly, determinedly refusing to ask him what he meant.

He told her, anyhow, as he drew on his cigarette and squatted down at the edge of the shaft.

'That tunnel you're so busy playing around with obviously yielded nothing.'

Frazer's violet-blue eyes sparked angrily, and she felt an impotent rage in her heart. He spoke so callously – so carelessly. Yet he knew who had opened that tunnel and he knew why the work had stopped – and he was pretending it had stopped because there was nothing there and there was not likely to be anything one foot further in. She said, her voice shaking slightly, 'You think you know, don't you?'

'I do know, Kate.' He looked at her hard as if he were challenging her to contradict him.

She wanted to say, 'You don't know a thing. My father would never have told you a thing – whatever he had found – and even if you hadn't killed him.' Instead she retorted fiercely, 'This drive's hardly been opened yet,' then turned her shoulder to him and began chipping again, aware that her limbs were trembling.

She knew he hadn't gone away, but she acted as if he had, and after a few minutes he said, 'You're certainly not playing, are you, Kate?'

'Not playing what?' she asked without turning. She had a feeling he was teasing her in some sophisticated way she couldn't understand, and her throat felt dry.

'I just mean you're not playing,' he repeated. 'In fact, you're dead serious about this opal search of yours. And I thought you'd come to Wandalilli for a story. So what's happened? Don't tell me you've got hooked after so short a time – and having found nothing.'

'I'm not going to tell you anything,' said Frazer, her

75

hands busy.

'I see. Measure for measure ... Well, it was a purely rhetorical question.'

Out of the corner of her eye she saw him straighten and stand for a moment, and then walk away.

For minutes after he had gone, she went on mechanically chipping, but her mind was seething. He rubbed her up the wrong way all the time – upset her – made her thoughts go haywire. She hated him – that went without saying – and yet when he was about, that very hatred, that had always been like a clear coloured thread woven into her mind, became something fluid, elusive. And now, as she chipped into the opal dirt, her attention kept wandering away. She should have been concentrating so carefully to hear a different sound as the pick dug into the soft pinkish white clay, but instead – instead, she kept seeing an image of Jay Dexter's face on the shadowed wall of the tunnel, and remembering the roughness of his unshaved chin against her cheek. And she could hear his voice casually, drawlingly, calling her 'Kate'.

Suddenly she let the pick drop. It was stifling hot, she couldn't concentrate, and she felt there was going to be a storm of some sort. Anyhow, it was time to go over to the camp for lunch ...

While they ate salad and fruit and drank cups of scalding tea, Caryl complained, 'It's so hot – I thought summer was over—'

'It's going to storm,' Frazer said. 'It'll clear the air and we'll all feel better.'

Caryl wasn't persuaded. 'Maybe. But I'm more and more convinced that Dexter man was right – if there'd been anything worth finding here, someone would have found it. Don't you agree, Rex?'

Rex didn't answer. He raked a hand through his long dark hair and lifted his shoulders. His eyes were on Frazer.

'Frazer knows something we don't. What is it, Frazer? Is there an Aladdin's cave under the ground on the hill?'

Frazer sighed inwardly. 'Nobody can be certain about opals – about whether or not you'll find them. You hear something and you follow it up, and you just hope.'

Caryl's green eyes were sceptical.

'What did *you* hear, then?'

'Nothing definite enough to impress you,' said Frazer unhappily. She reached for the billy and poured herself another mug of tea and wished Caryl would let it alone. Nothing was going to persuade her to tell them about her father – his hopes, his tragedy. Torture wouldn't drag the story from her. She didn't really know why she felt so strongly about this. It was as if there were things she didn't know herself – and deep, deep down was the fear that in the telling something might vanish. She looked up at Caryl and said with sudden decision, 'If you're really fed up, you can forget the whole thing and go. I'll understand.'

Rex said in a deadly quiet voice, 'Oh yes, Frazer will understand – now I've got the shaft cleared out for her.'

Caryl ignored him. 'And what would *you* do, Frazer?'

Frazer shrugged. 'Stay on. I haven't anything better to do just now.'

'There!' Caryl turned to Rex. 'I told you it wouldn't matter to Frazer if we opted out!'

Rex didn't do any more work that day. He and Caryl got on the motorbike and went into town.

'We'll be back,' he assured Frazer, an odd expression in his eyes. 'Don't work too hard while we're away.' Frazer looked away from him, her heart sinking. She wished heartily that Caryl had never brought him along.

As it happened she didn't do any more work herself either. The air was so heavy and oppressive, she tidied up the camp and then wandered about listlessly. Far out on the horizon which had darkened to a heavy purplish grey, there were streaks of lightning and distant almost soundless thunder seemed to make the earth tremble even here. Frazer was on edge, and watched nervily as the storm moved gradually towards Wandalilli. She didn't

77

like storms, and she was afraid of lightning. The iron-stone pebbles that were scattered over the ground seemed to her to assume an unearthly sheen as if they were answering the lightning that played with such terrifying abandon overhead. Frazer retreated inside her tent despite the heat so as not to see, and, when big drops of rain began to pelt down on the fly, she tried to persuade herself that it would soon be over. From her pack she produced with shaking hands her poverty pot – as her father had always called it – the marmite jar in which she had kept for years those two stones he had given her at their last meeting. But before she could even look for comfort and distraction in their beautiful fiery faces, the most tremendous sheet of lightning and a deafening clap of thunder straight overhead had reduced her to helpless fear.

She sat shivering and tense in the light of the small lamp she had lit, and presently forced herself to raise and look through the flap. Rain still came down in huge drops and it was almost night-dark until without warning another streak of lightning ripped open the sky, illuminating the plains so brightly that she could see the iron-stone pebbles wink and jump heavenwards, their shadows moving violently.

Frazer covered her eyes. The rain pelted down harder, a small branch fell, jerked at the tent fly, and slipped to the ground. She turned away and with shaking hands put her opals back in the poverty pot, thrust it into her pack, and without thinking, began to struggle into her waterproof windjacket and to pull on the boots she had earlier discarded. Her red helmet, upside down beside the bedding roll, was snatched up hastily, and then she was outside in the rain, running, with her eyes half closed to where her bike stood under a tree.

Vroom-vroom! She had the motor going and she was bolting across the flat, her mind so sick and frightened it held nothing. She was driven purely by instinct, not by any rational thought.

She shot along by the river, and ahead of her like a

beacon she saw a yellow light shining, while around her great drops of rain splashed dust up and turned it into red mud. The bike skidded a little and she could feel the thumping of her heart. She hated and despised herself for being so afraid of electrical storms, and yet she couldn't help it. Not to be able to control your mind because of your body's uncontrollable reaction to something external was terrible, and quite incomprehensible to anyone who had never experienced it. Frazer had only this one fear, and when it was a bad storm she all but lost her reason. When she was six years old – shortly after her mother had died – she had seen a tree split down the middle by lightning, and for some reason she had been convinced her father was standing underneath it. She had screamed and screamed, and then – he had come walking towards her and caught her up in his arms and she had lost consciousness . . . Right now, Frazer didn't even know where she was going except that her sights were set on that yellow light that showed waveringly through the deluge, the only landmark in the black dark except when the demoniacal lightning flooded the plain and set the ironstone pebbles laughing and leaping.

If only she could reach that light before the storm got her!

Head down, rain pouring from her red helmet, she rode her bike through the trees, and then – wham! – she was caught in the monstrous yawning mouth of the heavens as light and fire seemed to pour down, liquid, roaring, omnivorous . . .

Her mouth opened and she screamed at the top of her voice and her bike died beneath her.

Then someone was there, her arms were around a human form and she was sobbing like a little child. *'Don't cry, baby,'* her father had said, *'I'm here – I'm here – everything's all right.'* She raised her wet face and her sight came back – or had her eyes been closed? – and with a sharp shock she found she was staring into the scarcely discernible face of Jay Dexter.

'My God!' His hands gripped her shoulders hard

through the windjacket. 'What's got into you, Kate, to be riding around in a storm like this? I was coming down to see if everything was all right—'

Something snapped back into place quite literally in Frazer's mind, she actually felt it physically. And she said instantly and as though it were perfectly true, 'Of course everything's all right. It was just – my tent was coming adrift. I thought I'd shelter in – in the men's quarters.'

There was a second's silence. Then he said slowly and threateningly, 'No, you don't, Kate. You'll come back to the homestead with me. Your two mates haven't come back, have they?'

'Not yet,' she said, shivering with reaction now, and praying there would be no more lightning, no more ear-splitting thunder to throw her mind into turmoil again. 'They'll come when the storm's over.'

'They won't be back tonight,' he said, and she heard the cynicism in his voice. 'From the way they were playing around earlier on today I should think they'd have found some excuse even without the weather for staying in town till tomorrow.'

Frazer was silent. He didn't miss much, even if he didn't visit the camp every day now ... They were moving now, through the pouring rain. He was guiding the bike with one hand while the other kept a hold on her arm as if to guide her. Presently she remarked with an attempt at bravado, 'I don't like storms much. I always feel like an emu chick whose eggshell has broken open too soon when all that fire pours down and all that – all that bombardment goes on.'

'Is that how you see it?' he asked clinically, then added in a softer tone, 'It's a pretty fierce storm tonight anyhow.'

'Yes. But I'll be all right now. I'll – I'll go back—'

'I thought your tent was coming adrift.'

'I can sleep in one of the others,' she said swiftly.

'We're nearly home,' he said, ignoring her. 'And if you don't like storms you'll be better off with a roof over your head.'

She wished she could have insisted, but she couldn't. Even though he was – who he was – Jay Dexter. Yet she couldn't make herself say thank you, or even that it was kind of him. Because she knew he was far from being a kind man . . .

'First thing you'd better do is take a hot bath,' he said when they reached the yellow light and the shelter of the wide verandah where Frazer stood dripping and he stood dripping too. She looked at him once, very quickly, and then she looked away again as if she feared he had found out something intimate about her. 'But he couldn't have heard me scream,' she tried to assure herself. 'Not in all that noise. And I probably didn't scream nearly as loudly as I thought.' She pulled off her helmet and tossed back her tawny hair that was dripping wet at the ends, and when he held out his hands for her jacket, her violet eyes met his briefly and accidentally. She hadn't the slightest idea what he was thinking. His hand touched hers as he took the jacket, and he said, 'You're cold . . . Have you eaten tonight?'

She shook her head. 'It doesn't matter. I'm not hungry.'

'Well, since I haven't eaten either you might as well dine with me as starve . . . Go get yourself into a good hot bath now and I'll see if I can find some clothes for you to put on. Barbara generally leaves a few things behind.'

Frazer swallowed, her eyes widening. 'Isn't she – isn't your sister here?'

'No, Kate. Her husband came and collected her the other day. So there's just you and me and my housekeeper Dolly.' He moved to take her arm, but she jerked away. What was she letting herself in for? she wondered. He didn't touch her again but told her with slight amusement, 'Just round the corner there's a bedroom that opens on to the verandah. You can use that, and the bathroom next to it. Drop your wet things on the floor somewhere – Dolly will collect them later on. I'm going to shower and change too. We'll meet when we're more respectable.'

He left her abruptly at the corner of the verandah, and

Frazer went in the door he had indicated and switched on a light after fumbling for a few seconds. It was strange to be in a real house again and she looked about her curiously while she stripped off her dripping jeans and shift, having first ascertained that there was a white towelling robe hanging on the back of the door. It was a large uncluttered room, with a floor of polished hardwood and a couple of mats. The walls were painted off-white, the bedspread was patterned in wavering lines of black and white, the curtains were of plain coarse linen. The furniture was cedar, old-fashioned, and complemented by a big oval wall mirror framed in carved cedar.

Frazer, slipping hastily into the towelling robe and belting it tightly, caught sight of herself in that mirror and thought she looked a sorry sight. Despite her tan, her face looked almost ashen – and that was the effect of sheer fright. And she didn't have any make-up to hide it. She rarely used make-up, though Aunt Helen had bought her a beautiful kit in Sydney a few weeks ago – eye-shadow, stuff for her lashes which were thick and darkish anyhow, several shades of lipstick, cream to put on at night – Frazer hadn't bothered to examine half of it. She wasn't all that interested, and besides she had been too wrapped up in planning her Wandalilli expedition. Now, ridiculously, incomprehensibly, she wished she had that kit here – to hide herself.

She turned away from the mirror and went into a short hallway that was softly lit from the far end. She found the bathroom – small, with dark blue and white tiles, and two big soft towels hanging on the chrome rail. She half filled the big white bath, discarded the robe, and slid into the water, and oh, it was heavenly! There was scented soap that hadn't been used, and a towelling mitt that looked brand new, and she scrubbed and soaked – and washed her hair as well, it was too good an opportunity to miss – and listened to the rain on the roof as she luxuriated.

Her only regret was that when this was over, she had to face *him* again. She would so much sooner have gone straight to bed with a glass of warm milk, and slept.

Her face was still pale when she got back into the robe, wrapped a towel turban-like around her head, and padded quietly back to the bedroom. He had said he'd see if he could find her some clothes to put on. She hoped it would be slacks and not a linen shirtwaister or something she'd feel a positive fool in, and look like she was playing somebody's auntie in a school breaking up play.

She had closed the bedroom door behind her – the lamp was still on – before she saw what had been laid out on the bed. And then she gasped and for a second wanted to giggle. Tiny black panties, a black bra, and a dress that looked Asiatic – thin soft cotton in a pattern of green and blue and made with the utmost simplicity. A couple of girls at school had made evening dresses that way the material folded across, a bound slit for the neck, the sides stitched part way down on the outside, about eight inches in from the selvedge, the hem tapered up at the sides so as not to drag. The bra was too large and she discarded it, but had got into the panties and was wriggling into the dress when an appalling thought suddenly struck her. *What was all this about?* What was she dressing for? Why was she being handed clothes that just couldn't possibly belong to his sister Barbara?

She had dropped her towelling turban and as her head emerged through the neck of the dress she saw herself in the mirror, her tawny hair tangled and dark with water. What had he said that first early morning at the shaft – about depending for his breakfast conversation on – on liberated girls who found him sufficiently sympathetic and attractive to form a temporary alliance? Frazer's violet eyes darkened. Was that what he was expecting of *her*? With a final wriggle she pulled the dress over her hips. Well, she had to wear something, but she would very soon make it clear to him that *she* didn't find him either sympathetic or attractive. But oh! – to think she had fallen into his trap like some stupid gullible little girl!

The soft cotton dress lay caressingly against her thighs, and touched her calves gently as she moved across the room on bare feet – shoes were not provided. In the mirror she could see the pointed shape of her breasts, and as she turned a little, the line of her slender waist, the curve of her buttocks. She saw her cheeks flame and snatching up the towel, she began to rub her hair vigorously. His sister Barbara's clothes! That was a likely story. It was perfectly plain he kept these clothes for – for any liberated girl who would accept his invitation.

'So now what do I do?' Frazer asked herself, staring round a little wildly. She groped in the drawer of the cedar chest in the hope of finding a comb, but drew a blank. She ran her fingers through her hair to get it into some sort of order. 'I'll get back into my wet jeans and shirt, and my boots,' she thought feverishly. 'I'll sneak out and find my motorbike and ride back to the tent and forget about the storm. That won't worry me now, I swear. It will be better than staying here . . .'

She had just realized that her wet clothes had been taken away when there was a light tap at the door. Her heart jumped sky high and began to pound so loudly she could no longer hear the torrential rain that still thundered on the roof.

Tensely, she went to the door and opened it, ready to demand her clothes.

CHAPTER FIVE

HER mouth closed with the words unspoken. It wasn't Jay Dexter she found herself confronting. It was a fat and rather elderly aboriginal woman – Dolly – who smiled widely and looked her over with wholehearted approval.

'You had 'nough bathtub now, Kate? Boss wait'm longa dining-room. S'pose you foller longa me.'

Frazer's resolutions collapsed. Helplessly she followed, desperately trying to smooth her nearly dry hair, aware of the absurdity of her bare feet.

She had a short reprieve when she reached the dining-room, for Dexter was standing with his back to her pouring himself a whisky – she could smell it – at the sideboard. He apparently didn't hear her come into the room on her bare feet, and she waited silently, her lower lip caught between her teeth, taking it all in and – wondering.

It was a smallish room with cedar walls on which were hung some framed photographs of horses. The narrow rectangular table was set with place mats of coarse linen, silverware, and, surprisingly, an old-fashioned brass candelabrum holding three candles, all of them lit and providing the only illumination in the room. An earth-brown lidded casserole dish stood on a thick mat at one end of the table, there was a board piled with thick slices of home-made bread, a silver dish of butter, plain white plates, and a glass water jug flanked by tumblers with heavy bases.

The whisky poured, the crystal decanter restoppered, Jay Dexter turned leisurely, and their eyes met. His were black, remote, faintly quizzical, and they took her in very quickly. The unpleasant thought sprang into her mind that he was aware of every stitch she had on under the long dress, that he wanted to see how she shaped up in the gear he had provided, and she felt perversely glad that her hair was bedraggled enough to spoil her image.

'Feeling better?' he asked carelessly.

She nodded, and he raised the whisky glass to his lips, then set it down again. 'Whisky for you too, Kate? Or are you warmed through? I'm sorry I don't have sherry to offer you.'

Frazer said stiffly, 'It's quite all right, thank you, I don't drink whisky. Or sherry,' she added, then rather wished she hadn't admitted to it. Despite herself, one hand strayed nervously to her hair. *His* hair, thick and dark and damp, was perfectly groomed. He wore dark pants and a casual, high-necked pull-on shirt of soft ivory-coloured cotton. And black shoes of soft-looking leather. Frazer glanced down. She could see her bare feet and feel the silky wood of the floor cool beneath them.

'I hope your toes aren't cold,' he said, following her glance. 'Barbara doesn't appear to have left any footgear around, though I don't expect her slippers would fit you in any case. You look quite charming, by the way – I scarcely recognized you for a moment. Like some princess in a story book.'

He spoke with faint mockery, and the colour flared briefly in her pale cheeks. 'Princess' was like the flick of a whip on a raw nerve. She didn't want to hear 'princess' from him! She watched half angrily through her lashes while he swallowed down his whisky, and then he said crisply, 'Well then, sit down, Kate.'

He moved to the table and pulled out a chair for her and she slid into it without a word. She would eat – why not? – and then he would find out, the minute he made a move in the wrong direction, that she was not that sort of a girl.

She flinched as she felt the warmth of his hands on her head smoothing her hair.

'I didn't provide you with a comb, did I? I might have guessed that woman-like you'd have washed your hair. It's got quite a sheen to it now you've got the dust out.'

Frazer sat as though frozen, and felt his fingers delicately lift the hair from the back of the neck. And then –

86

as she was wondering why she was mad enough to sit here, was ready to leap out of the chair if he should— Then he moved away casually and took the lid from the casserole. Her nostrils quivered. Whatever was in that pot, it smelled delicious, and she *was* hungry. After all, she'd done some hard physical work today. He didn't ask her if she fancied taking a portion but ladled out a good helping of vegetables and beef on to one of the white plates and handed it to her.

'Dolly's speciality – stew,' he remarked. 'Help yourself to bread, Kate.'

His own serving piled lavishly on the plate, he took the chair opposite her, and she glanced up and caught his dark eyes on her watchfully. His attitude seemed to say, 'Relax', and there was a flicker of impatience in the tilt of his wide mouth as he pushed the bread towards her, though she could quite easily have reached it herself. He found her schoolgirlishly gauche, she thought. He didn't know she was edgy because she was a wake-up to him and his – strategy. Well, he would see soon enough that she had her share of *savoir faire*.

A fresh downpour started as they began to eat, and it was a good enough excuse for not talking. The stew was good, and so was the bread, and Frazer did the meal full justice, and poured herself a tumbler of water with as much composure as if she were in a restaurant sharing a table with a stranger. That, for the time being, she decided, was the best way to look at it. It wasn't all that difficult either, because the Jay Dexter who sat opposite her in the candlelight was so different from the man she had several times crossed swords with in blazing sunlight, his background the harsh plains, the glare of the limitless sky. She glanced at him fleetingly once or twice and was baffled. He was ignoring her, concentrating completely on his meal. The soft candlelight made his tanned skin glow warmly, and he looked freshly shaved and infinitely civilized in his casual but expensive-looking shirt. His mouth drew her eyes again and again – not because of what had happened the other night, but because of the curve of it. It wasn't the hard male mouth typical of the opal miners she remembered from a childhood spent among them, and it wasn't a noncommittal everyday sort of mouth like her Uncle Frank's. As he paused in his eating to reach for the water jug, she thought suddenly, 'Isn't there a word – sensual? Isn't that how you'd describe a mouth like that?' She took another quick look and was sure it was, and then she thought with quickening heart, 'What happens when we've finished eating?'

What happened was that he pushed back his chair with a murmured excuse and moved to the sideboard where he put coffee to percolate, and turned up two of half a dozen small dark brown coffee cups that stood on a tray.

When he turned back he stood looking down at her and not trying to conceal it in the least, and the curious thought came to her that perhaps he found her something of a stranger too. She supposed that in their encounters in the open air she had so often been assertive, wild, defiant – rather the way she had been at fourteen when she had first come to Aunt Helen and had so appalled her. In here – in this room – she was subdued, silent, like – like a caged animal. Did he think that? Or did he see her, dressed up in the charming gown, as a possible – love conquest?

She jumped slightly when he said abruptly, 'The storm's clipped your wings, Kate. Where's all your aggressiveness gone tonight? Or is it hunger that's kept you so quiet?'

She said nothing. Her violet-blue eyes looked back at him warily and beneath the blue and green dress, her heart had begun an agitated hammering.

'I think you're a girl who doesn't like to be in a cage,' he said consideringly. 'Is that why you choose to live in a tent, to shovel dirt and rocks and to career around the countryside on a motorbike?' He paused, and the blackness of his eyes bored into her intently.

Frazer thought, 'So that's how he sees me.' Somehow it was not at all a flattering picture, and it didn't endear him to her, but she shrugged as if she couldn't care less what he thought about her.

'No one looking at you now would suspect you of being such a fire-eater and a harum-scarum. You're all femininity now we've got you out of that aggressively unisex gear and into something more becoming.'

That was a little too much. Frazer's cheeks flared with angry colour, then paled again as she tried in vain to find something to say to put him in his place. She hadn't yet contributed a word to this conversation, and now her mind seemed to be in too much of a turmoil for her to sort out any phrases. And that exact moment, too, a sheet of lightning illuminated the window and her eyes closed involuntarily and her whole body stiffened.

'You're scared of storms too, aren't you?' he remarked conversationally. 'You'd rather spend a night under my roof than down in your tent alone with the lightning.'

When she opened her eyes he had turned away to deal with the coffee and she saw him pour something from a squat bottle into each of the two cups.

'A dash of Benedictine,' he said with a faint smile as he handed her one of the small cups, then added flatly, matter-of-factly, 'You don't like me, do you, Kate?'

Frazer said, 'No.'

'I wonder why not.' He didn't sit down at the table again but stood with his back to the sideboard, his face in shadow. Frazer sipped her coffee and gasped a little at the fiery taste of the liqueur. She wondered how it would be if she said quite simply, I hate you because you are my father's – murderer. Her eyes met his and she blinked quickly, as if he could read her mind. Murderer is a strong word.

He drank half his coffee. 'Now how about telling me about yourself, Kate? It's a very one-sided conversation we're having – very heavy going for me.'

Frazer took another swallow. Where was all that *savoir faire*? All she could think of to say was, 'I'm Cathleen Frazer Madigan, and you killed my father because you wouldn't take the trouble.' But if she said it now, she knew with a sudden feeling of cold in the pit of her stomach, she would burst into tears – childish tears. And he

– of course he would explain it all away with his arms about her even. He was the kind of man who was never at a loss – 'I didn't know the gun was loaded' – and she wouldn't believe a word he said. 'No, she didn't want to hear. And besides – besides, there was some other reason that she couldn't quite get hold of why she couldn't say it to him. Not yet, anyhow, not yet . . .

Aware that he was waiting for her to say something, she managed with flat roughness, 'I don't know what you mean.'

She heard him sigh. 'Now come on, Kate, you can do better than that. It's not the first time you've been asked a similar question by an interested male – and I'll swear that somewhere behind that determinedly farouche exterior you've a set of well learned comfortable social habits. So don't let me down.'

His sudden smile alarmed her, and she sipped again, and refused to look at him. All the thoughts in her head were floating about like the fragments of a shattered mosaic – out of place, meaningless. This, she sensed, must be the preliminary gambit to the game of love Jay Dexter was looking for, and she had no idea how to deal with it. She was, quite simply, too unpractised, too naïve. Nothing she had ever learned on the opal fields or at boarding school had taught her to fence verbally with a man like Jay Dexter. She thought ridiculously, longingly, of her black jeans, her mulberry shirt, her boots – of the dusty toil in the shaft, the burning bright sunlight that hid nothing. Out there – out there she knew how to deal with life. But here, in the candlelight, alone with a man who wasn't the Jay Dexter she had grown accustomed to, it was a different matter.

She said suddenly and with a kind of desperation, 'You know all about me. I'm – I'm fossicking for opals.' She stopped as abruptly as she had begun and ran the tip of her tongue over her top lip and looked straight at him.

His wide mouth curved up at one end and he shook his head.

'That's a lie, Kate. You're not just fossicking for opals.

You're fossicking for something else. What is it? A story? A dream?'

Frazer blinked, and drained her coffee cup. Somehow, he had hit on a deep truth. She wasn't just fossicking for opals – because opals were far more than stones to her. And to unearth here, on Wandalilli, the one beautiful perfect stone that her father had spent his whole life seeking – that would be to realize a dream. But it wasn't something she wanted to explain to Jay Dexter, so she told him sturdily, 'Just opals – that's all I'm looking for. Opals. They're special enough, opals, hidden in the dark for centuries. And you bring them into the light and polish them, and they shine like fire and stars and—' She stopped, wondering why she had said that, and embarrassed by the curiosity of his regard.

'So you've fallen in love with a precious stone, have you,' he commented. 'What a waste of passion! And you're how old?'

'Nineteen – almost,' said Frazer, shaken and somehow angry.

His eyes mocked her. 'Well, there's hope for you yet ... Do you want more coffee?'

'No, thank you. And' – the words seemed forced from her – 'I'll go back to the camp now.'

His black eyes narrowed incredulously. 'My God, you're a stupid child! Be thankful you're here, under a roof with dry clothes, and a comfortable bed waiting for you.'

'The others will be back,' she said furiously.

'Be your age, Kate,' he said impatiently. 'They'll be back tomorrow if the storm's over. Your girl friend doesn't share your passion for opals, in any case, does she? She prefers to gallop around and a bit of fun with your bearded friend.'

Frazer flushed. 'Well, what's wrong with that?' she demanded, and added, not having the least idea what she was going to say, 'Anyhow, Rex – Rex wants to come back.'

'That I'll believe,' he said after a moment. 'So do you

give in to reason? You'll have another screaming fit if I drop you down at the camp tonight. There's no guarantee that the frightening part of the storm's all behind us yet – quite apart from the dark and the floods of water you're going to have to deal with all on your own.'

Frazer got up from her chair. 'Then I'll go to bed now – right away.'

She had actually forgotten her conviction that he had designs on her virtue when he moved unexpectedly in front of her and said softly, 'Shall I kiss you good night, Kate?'

He put his hands on her upper arms, and she could feel their warmth through the fine soft stuff of the blue and green dress. Her heart began to hammer. So it was happening – she had known it would – when she got into those black undies ... And now his eyes were running over the length of her and she shivered and wanted to hide herself, and she gasped out an emphatic, 'No! I'm not – I'm not—' Her voice faltered and failed her. 'Not a liberated girl,' she had wanted to say.

He didn't let her go. His dark fiery eyes were on her face now – compelling her eyes, then moving to her lips. He said even more softly, 'It's a pity. Out of your bikie clothes you're a very attractive girl, Kate.' His hands shifted their position. One was against her back between her shoulder blades, drawing her closer. The other was on her hair, smoothing it back from her forehead, and at the same time forcing her to keep her head up, to look back at him. 'I think I'm going to kiss you, Kate,' he murmured. 'I think I must—'

It seemed to Frazer there was a long pause then, while she stayed as completely motionless as if she were paralysed, aware of the beating of her heart making small jerky movements within her breast, feeling her bosom close against the warmth of him, feeling his hand pressing hard against her back.

'Maybe you think a gentleman shouldn't force his attentions on a woman, Kate,' he said almost inaudibly. 'But it's going to happen this time – for all of us there has to be – a beginning—' The final words were scarcely breathed out when his mouth was hard on hers and she felt herself freeze in his arms – go stiff as a piece of petrified wood, though her heart was still hammering frantically. And then – at the very moment she felt something within herself let go – he put her away from him, and she stood, arms limp, cheeks white, body trembling.

'So you really dislike me,' he said coolly. He turned away, back to the sideboard, and poured himself another whisky. 'You'd better get off to bed.'

He spoke so carelessly – so carelessly, as though to a child. As though she and her kisses didn't matter the least little bit to him . . .

She locked her bedroom door. Neither he nor Dolly had put any night things there for her, and she wrapped herself in the towelling robe and got under the sheet and the single soft blanket and lay awake in the dark for a long time. Listening to the rain that still fell, her mind returning again and again, despite her resistance, to that uncompleted kiss. She lay rigid and unrelaxed, agonized by her thoughts, and by the unaccustomed unease of her body – her virginal body that until now had been the innocent unawakened body of a schoolgirl, and had tonight from a man's touch blossomed into pain and into something that she recognized dimly as desire.

'No,' she told herself, anguished. 'No – never. He is the man whose callousness killed my father.' Besides, he had only been amusing himself with her. And he had let her go because – her mind shrank from the thought – because after all he found her unamusing.

She tried to switch the train of her thoughts. 'Tomorrow I'll work on the second tunnel. The shaft's clear at last. I'll find a patch of opal under the roof – my father was certain it was there—'

Suddenly it was all utterly meaningless, and she stopped her determined monologue with sick weariness. 'Who am I?' she wondered. 'Why have I come to Wandalilli?' She felt filled with a mistrust of many things. Her future that had once seemed so clear cut and simple was now like shattered glass. Jay Dexter had become a hard and compelling reality that frightened her. With him, she would have to come to terms some time, for a variety of reasons. It seemed that all the dreams and ambitions she had fostered in herself at school were no more real or lasting than coloured bubbles. They belonged with a childishness that because of *him* was now dropping from her. They were fantasies that had been an escape from the world of reality. Yet she rebelled at the notion that her search for the opal had become a pretence. It could not be so. Tomorrow when she woke her work would still be there waiting for her. Good sense would take over the spell be broken. The pieces of glass would fall into place again and she would wonder why she had ever let that man disturb her.

She woke to bright sunlight, and knew with relief that by now he would have gone out on the run to see what damage the storm had done. She found the aboriginal housekeeper, Dolly, got back into her comfortable familiar clothes, had breakfast on the verandah – succulent steak and two eggs – and in no time was off on her motorbike, riding down by the river towards the tents that looked as if they'd taken something of a beating in the storm.

There were broken branches and leaves everywhere, but the sun was hot and the red earth was steaming as the rain water was sucked back into the blue of the heavens. The cockatoos and parrots were noisy in the trees, and she could hear the song of the river and her heart lifted. In no time at all everything would be as it had been – the memory of last night would fade away and disappear.

The only fly in the ointment was that she hadn't a hope in hell of avoiding *him* for ever. Not while she stayed here.

Rex and Caryl came riding back from Minning Minning during the morning. They talked about the storm, and Rex inspected the tents and then strolled up to take a look at the shaft, while Frazer helped Caryl unpack the foodstuffs they had brought back with them.

Caryl asked with a rather airy unconcern, 'Was it awful here all by yourself last night, Fraze? I remember at school you used to have fits if there was lightning.' Then without waiting for an answer, she hurried on, 'I'm sorry for deserting you, but—'

'Oh, that's all right,' said Frazer quickly, inwardly trying to make up her mind whether or not to tell Caryl what had happened. But she didn't want to talk about it, and Caryl wasn't worried, so what was the point. 'I wouldn't have expected you to come back in a storm like that.'

Caryl looked at her over a bag of peaches that were tumbling on to the ground, and her green eyes were bright. 'As a matter of fact, we just nearly didn't come back at all. We just nearly got lured away by the bright lights of Minning Minning – all two of them,' she concluded, wryly.

Frazer frowned a little, uncertain whether she was serious or not.

Caryl said, 'I can see what you're thinking, Fraze. You think Rex and I shared a bed at the motel. Well, we didn't, so stop looking so disapproving. He wanted it, of course, and – don't ask me why I said no, I hardly know myself except I suddenly got kind of – scared. Maybe if he hadn't been so set on coming back here to the opals – and—' She stopped and gave Frazer an oddly veiled look and Frazer felt faint shock. She was certain Caryl had been about to say 'and *you*'. But surely not, surely she was imagining it. And imagining too the little rift that seemed to be developing between herself and Caryl. Partly because of Rex, undoubtedly. It seemed strange that already there was a man complicating their lives, spoiling their schoolday friendship. She wanted to assure Caryl that Rex didn't like her, but she was not altogether convinced of that herself, and to say that she didn't like him might be tactless, because Caryl was so clearly enamoured of him. Eventually, on the principle that it is better to say too little than too much, she didn't follow the matter any further.

After lunch they cleared up the damage done by the storm about the camp site – removed broken branches and the myriad leafy twigs that had been stripped from the gum trees; aired and dried and re-erected the tents – none of which had been damaged, fortunately – and washed the groundsheets.

Then Rex said, 'What do you think, Frazer? Shall we put in a bit of work at the mine this afternoon or wait till it's less mucky tomorrow?'

Frazer gave a slight start and coloured guiltily. She hadn't even been up to the shaft to take a look at it! What was the matter with her? She said evasively, 'How was it when you looked earlier on?'

He shrugged. 'Didn't look as bad as I expected, but I didn't go down. Come up and take a look. Caryl can get on with the housework,' he added patronizingly.

'But—' began Frazer, and Caryl said sharply, 'Oh, go along, for goodness' sake. *I* don't want to look at the filthy old shaft. I can just imagine the horrid mess it will be – mud and puddles.' And she turned away.

Frazer bit her lip, then, helplessly, walked away with Rex. After a few paces he remarked, 'I'll bet you didn't weather out the storm all alone in your little tent last night, Frazer. What did you do? Run up to the homestead and persuade the big boss to take you in?' He looked sideways at her as he spoke, his light-coloured eyes knowing. 'I reckon you're not all that tough underneath your swagger, Fraze – you're just as feminine and soft as Caryl. You're better looking too.'

Frazer gritted her teeth. What sort of a man had Caryl fallen in love with? She said tightly, 'I don't want compliments from you, and what I did last night was my own business. I'm not asking you what *you* did last night.'

'I'll tell you if you like,' he said offhandedly. 'Caryl put it to me – not quite in words – that if I'd promise to forget about this opal business, she'd—'

'I don't want to hear,' Frazer interrupted sharply. She put on pace and moved rapidly ahead, and reached the shaft before he did. She felt full of helpless rage that Caryl had fallen for a man like that ... There were a few puddles of water in the mine, but it was not as bad as she had imagined it would be, and she was pleased they had shifted the mullock before it became heavy and sticky with water. She clambered down, slipping a little, and looked inside the drive. She glanced up as Rex's shadow fell across her own.

'It's dry enough inside the tunnel,' she said coolly. 'But it's too late to do anything today – we might as well leave it till tomorrow.'

'If you say so,' Rex agreed. 'Meanwhile you might clue me up a bit more. What happens, for instance, if I drive the pick right into this seam you were telling me about? Do I shatter the lot and lose a fortune?' He reached down a hand to her and after a slight hesitation she took it and let him help her clamber out. His hand was work-roughened and it was strong, and he still held on to her fingers when she stood beside him. Quite suddenly she definitely didn't like this physical contact with him. She pulled her hand away and without thinking, wiped it on the seat of her jeans, then began to answer his question as though nothing had happened and ignoring the malicious amusement at the back of his eyes.

She told him a few basic facts about using with care the chisel point of the pick – about feeling – about listening for a different sound. 'As for shattering, you're hardly likely to find a great chunk of opal or a piece a foot square! It will be in small stones, and of course you could ruin a single stone, and it could be a good one – or it could be potch. Did you know, by the way, that Australian opals are the hardest and most durable in the world? They face up well – they're not over-sensitive to the heat of the wheel.'

Rex listened, a curious little smile on his face. Then he nodded and screwed up his eyes, looking at her. 'I just don't get you, Frazer. I just don't see how you can have spent half your short life in that girls' school with Caryl and come out knowing the things you do. About opal mining,' he added after a fractional pause. 'And don't tell me your uncle took you fossicking in the holidays, because there's more to it than that.'

He was looking at her hard, and Frazer looked back. 'It's his eyes I don't like,' she thought. 'They're sort of – two-dimensional.' She remembered suddenly a man they'd called Black Jack on the opal fields. He'd had eyes like that, and he'd been caught out thieving another man's finds, and there'd been a fight. She'd seen it start up, and then her father had ordered, 'Frazer, you get off home and do some work on the wheel.' She had been eleven or twelve, and she had run fast because she'd been more horrified than fascinated. Later, her father had told her, 'Avarice is an ugly thing, Princess. And when a man has no feeling of mateship, then he's his own enemy.' 'It's why I don't like Rex,' she thought now, confusedly, and smiled at him faintly as if to cover it up.

She said lightly, 'You can amuse yourself guessing about me then, Rex, because I'm sure you wouldn't believe me if I *did* tell you the truth.'

Next day was hot and dry and windy, and Frazer was awake very early. She could feel the ground vibrating, and she knew it was horses. She struggled out of her sleeping bag and looked out from the tent. It was barely light and the ground was hazed with slowly lifting vapour. Clear cut as a red moon, the curve of the sun showed on the horizon, and the stockmen from Wandalilli were riding out over the plain on their horses. Frazer stood straining her eyes watching – searching.

Suddenly she knew she was looking for Jay Dexter amongst the men with their broad-brimmed hats and checked shirts and coloured neckerchiefs, all of them riding with long stirrups and an ease that came from practically living in the saddle. Abruptly, she turned away and reached for her boots. What did it matter to her where Jay Dexter was, so long as there was a good distance between him and her? She didn't want to see him

. . . She zipped up her boots and looked determinedly eastwards again, and watched as the sun pulled itself clear of the earth and emerged, dazzling, in a sky that was cloudless and faintly green. It was amazing how the rain had soaked away into the hungry earth or been drawn back into the heavens. A few more days, and it would be dusty again. But there could be new grasses springing up too. 'It will be good for the stock,' Frazer thought.

They breakfasted early. Frazer cut thick slices of the fresh bread, and cooked bacon and eggs and made a billy of tea. Caryl said she had a headache and was going to sit in the shade and do her nails and read a magazine. So Frazer washed the dishes, and Rex went on his own to the shaft.

'Have you got some aspirin, Caryl?'

Caryl looked up from the magazine, her face expressionless. 'Yes, thanks. Don't worry about me. I just haven't been bitten by the opal bug. You and Rex carry on.'

You and Rex. Frazer stood undecided, frowning, very much aware that for Caryl the whole thing was becoming an imposition. Then she sighed and turned away and went up to the shaft, wishing rather meanly that Caryl had never met Rex Byfield, that Robert had come instead.

Rex peered out at her from the drive. His face was covered with dirt and sweat, and Frazer reflected that he would be a lot more comfortable if he cut his hair and dispensed with the beard – but that was not for her to say. He didn't inquire about Caryl, he said, 'Come down and tell me if I'm doing the right thing.'

He was, of course. Watching him, she thought, 'He's learning quickly – he's a real opal miner. Keen, too.'

'Could I have missed anything?' he asked presently. 'Like to check over that pile of rubble I've knocked down before we shovel it out of the way, Fraze?'

Frazer grimaced. Rex was giving the orders now. *She* should have been the one who was chipping away at the roof of the drive – that was how she had always seen it.

This was *her* personal and private mission. But what was there to do about it? So after a second she began to do as Rex had said, although she knew in her heart that there would be nothing to find.

Time went by slowly. Rex worked away single-mindedly, and looking at him toiling, she thought dryly, 'It will be a pity if all that energy is for nothing – as it so easily could be.' It was a discomfiting thought. So short a while ago she had been absolutely certain they would make a find – they would strike that patch of precious opal her father had felt with a sixth sense would be there. Now, as though she were some disillusioned old hand, she saw Rex as a new chum about to receive his first hard lesson in frustration and disappointment, and she wondered if after it he would give the game away.

Presently she straightened her back. Her mind was too restless to allow her to stay fiddling here. Hard physical work would have held her, but not this – in this company.

'I've had enough. I'm going to take a swim in the river while there's still plenty of water in it,' she told Rex. 'It will have gone down again in a day or so.'

He looked up at her, his face speckled with the pinkish opal dirt. 'You're going to leave me all alone in this prospective Aladdin's cave? I'm surprised. I had the feeling you didn't trust me – Kate.'

Kate! She felt as though he had slapped her face.

'Don't call me Kate!' she flared. 'Frazer's the name.' Her words were accompanied by a swift and vivid mental image of herself – standing in the pile of mullock, booted feet apart, wearing black jeans, a shirt which needed washing; her hands filthy, her hair – so clean and shining a couple of nights ago – now dulled and limp. She flipped it back from her cheek impatiently, touched her tongue to her lips and tasted dirt. 'I'm not afraid to leave you alone. If you should strike opal, you're not going to gouge it all out of that roof in a couple of hours.'

'You know it all, don't you?' he marvelled, amused rather than otherwise at her flash of temper. 'One of these days—'

'You're going to get me to tell you the story of my life,' Frazer finished curtly for him. She turned her back and clambered as agilely as she could out of the shaft. She thought acidly, 'He's going to have to do some *really* hard work soon – when he's picked over all that bit of roof. He's going to have to extend that drive – and then he'll lose his enthusiasm.' As she marched down the slope she had a curiously certain feeling that Rex wasn't going to find anything. Not anything at all. And certainly not the Wandalilli Princess.

Caryl had gone into her tent and she put her head inside. 'How's the headache? Want to come down to the river for a swim?'

'No, thanks.' Caryl was looking pretty and feminine in a pale green dress and red sandals, and now she was painting her nails.

Frazer said carefully, so there would be no mistake, 'Rex is still slogging away in the mine.'

'Oh,' said Caryl indifferently. She obviously had no intention of joining him.

Frazer shrugged to herself as she went to fetch a towel and soap and her tape recorder. On impulse, she took a cotton dress that buttoned down the front to wear back when she was clean and fresh again. She could look feminine too, and she was a little tired of looking dirty and rough. But it was definitely not on Rex's account!

She found a deep and brimming hole in the river where before there had been no more than an adequate pool. She switched on her tape so she could listen to some classical music, and stripped off her clothes, leaving them under a tree on the bank. Then, stark naked, she slid into the water. It was not cold, because the sun shone on it with dazzling brightness, and after she had swum about for a while, she came back to the bank and reached for the soap and washed her hair, ducking under the water to rinse it. Then she swam again, letting it float across her naked shoulders. The thought drifted through her mind that she had forgotten to bring a comb, and that made her think of the other night at the homestead, and for the first time since then she allowed herself to go over in her mind everything that had happened then, in all the detail she could remember. She lay floating on her back, the water lapping gently against her ears, the sun on her face. Now and again she heard drifts of music, but mostly she heard nothing but her own thoughts, her eyes closed, the sunlight blood-red through her lids.

Who had that green and blue dress belonged to? she wondered. She simply couldn't believe it belonged to Jay Dexter's sister. Far more likely it had belonged to some girl who had been ready and eager to answer to the male in Jay Dexter, to swoon into his arms, to allow him to carry her to some couch and make love to her. While she, Cathleen Frazer Madigan, had been like a piece of wood in his arms. And her conversation over dinner—! Frazer rocked restlessly on the waters at the memory. She felt humiliated to think of it – she had contributed nothing – nothing! He would certainly never bother coming down to the camp again on her account. But then he never had. He had come only to intimidate her.

She felt both ashamed and subtly wounded by her own thoughts and by the memory of her own lack of sophistication. She wished – she wished she could justify herself somehow – fight back, hurt him. Tell him, 'In case you wondered at my coolness the other night, Mr. Dexter – it just happens I can't have any warm feelings for a man who doesn't know what mateship is – who is more or less a – a' – she hesitated in her mind over 'murderer', and flipped over on her face, opening her eyes.

As she did so, she saw with a shock that *he* had come through the trees, and now he stood on the bank in the sunlight, hands on his narrow hips, brows down and eyes narrowed as he gazed across the water at her.

Frazer felt she could have died. With her feet, she groped for the river bed, and she prayed that he couldn't see her nakedness through the water – her creamy body, ripple-marked by the sunlight. Shoulders exposed, she moved awkwardly, flusteredly, towards the bank where her clothes were, and where the tree shadows made the water more opaque. If he was a gentleman, she thought with futile anger, he'd have gone away instead of standing there, waiting.

He moved along the bank too. He said, 'I know you don't consider me a gentleman, Kate, but I assure you my manners are very nice indeed compared with what you could expect from one or two of my stockmen if they should catch you swimming here. In the nude,' he added, and she was sure his dark eyes could see right through the water, and instinctively she put her hands over her breasts. His nostrils were white, and there was a look of anger on his face.

Frazer opened her mouth, but could find nothing to say except, 'There aren't – there aren't any stockmen about—'

'There will be soon,' he said grimly. 'And you're certainly advertising your presence with that music blaring out like a siren song to attract the traveller.' He stopped and switched the tape off, almost viciously. 'It occurs to me you're so wide-eyed you don't even know when you're playing with fire. One of these days there's going to be a most terrific flare-up and you'll find out that fire burns. Now, get out of the water – and make yourself decent.'

He turned his back abruptly on Frazer's heightened colour, and walked a short distance away to stand in shadow and roll himself a cigarette. Shaken, she watched him for thirty seconds, and when he rapped out suddenly, 'Come along now – get moving!' she clambered hastily on to the bank, feeling the sunlight warm on her body. She was shivering, but it was certainly not with cold, and without waiting to dry herself, she dragged on her jeans and pulled the soiled tan cotton shirt over her head. And seeing how it clung to her wet bosom, regretted her haste. Her hair dripped water on her shoulders, and she gave it a quick and energetic rubbing with her towel. Then, sending a lightning glance at the man who still stood, back turned, blue smoke curling up from his cigarette, she grabbed up her underwear and bundled it up with the cotton dress and the towel, and sitting down on the ground, began to pull on her socks and boots.

Why on earth hadn't she put on the dress? she wondered futilely, uncomfortable in her dirty working gear. And she knew very well it had been defiance mixed with fear. She wasn't going to appear in – in female garb for Jay Dexter's benefit. For him she preferred the despised unisex gear . . . Her boots zipped up, she stood up warily, and at that moment he turned and came towards her. She felt his black eyes flick over her, saw the lift at the corners of his mouth that was anything but pleasant, and stooped for her clothes to hold them protectively, concealingly, in front of her.

He cocked his dark brows at her. 'No comb again, Kate?' he said, his voice hard, clipped. 'Here, have a loan of mine.' He reached into his hip pocket and offered it to her, but she didn't budge, except to toss back her head and say, 'No, thank you. I'm not going anywhere.'

His anger and impatience showed in the long line of his mouth. 'You act like a savage in every way. What's the point in cleaning yourself up, anyhow, if you're going to get back into those filthy and unbecoming clothes you affect? Now take this comb and tidy your hair at least.'

Frazer stepped aside as he thrust the comb almost menacingly at her, caught her foot on a stone, and dropped her towel as she grabbed awkwardly for the nearest thing – which was Jay Dexter. And then somehow or other he had hold of her, and whether she liked it or not he was – not kissing her, though she had leapt to the conclusion that that was what he was going to do – but dragging the comb hard again and again through the tangles of her hair.

Tears started to her eyes and she stood frightened almost out of her wits until finally he desisted. Her hair clung smoothly to her head and leafed against the pallor of her cheeks, and his eyes went to her lips and to the palpitating breast so revealingly outlined by the damp shirt.

He said with restrained fury, 'Someone should teach

you how to be a woman – before you learn the hard way.'

She hadn't the least idea what he meant, and her violet eyes, wide, blank, stayed fixed on him. Suddenly he let her go with some exclamation half beneath his breath, and stooped abruptly to pick up the things she had dropped.

'So you brought a dress along – but you're not going to wear it for my benefit. For your bearded friend, I suppose.'

Frazer's voice emerged husky, cracked. 'He's not my friend—'

His mouth relaxed a little. 'Well, take your things and get back to your tin of baked beans. What sort of progress are you making under the ground, anyhow?'

The beginning of a sob caught in Frazer's throat. Why, she had no idea. She took her clothes and her tape recorder and they began to walk together under the trees. She had the feeling he was offering, quite inexplicably, an olive branch. And she was uncertain whether or not to take it. She said neutrally, 'No progress. But we're still hoping.'

He grunted. They had reached the edge of the trees, and he stopped and put a hand on her shoulder so firmly that he was able to make her turn a little.

'What do you see over there, Kate?'

Frazer looked – and she saw a string of men on horseback coming over the plain in the direction of the homestead. She swallowed hard.

'I'd have been dressed before they came.'

'You might not have been. Next time you want to take a bath, you'd better come up to the house. You know where the bathroom is, and I'll tell Dolly to see it's left ready for your use.'

'No, thank you' was ungraciously on the tip or Frazer's tongue when he added, 'Bring your girl-friend along too, of course. I take it she's back?'

'Yes.' Frazer's heart had leapt a little. It might cheer Caryl up if she could go to the homestead and take a civilized bath whenever she wanted. 'What about Rex?' she heard herself ask almost aggressively. She looked up at him and saw his long mouth harden.

'Rex can rough it. He's old enough and ugly enough – and I didn't ask him to do what he's doing.'

'Nor me,' Frazer said. 'You never wanted me to come here.'

'That's right. I didn't, did I, Kate?' he agreed pleasantly. And with an enigmatic smile he walked casually away.

Frazer stood looking after him, frustrated and baffled.

CHAPTER SIX

She went straight to her tent when she reached the camp, intent only on getting out of her dirty clothes and into something fresh. She had taken it for granted without even thinking about the matter that Rex would still be in the shaft when suddenly she heard voices coming from Caryl's tent – Caryl's voice, Rex's voice. Frazer, struggling out of her shirt, heard,

'So you like opals better than me! Well, that's great, isn't it? I'm not even flesh and blood to you—'

'You're pretty cold flesh and blood,' Rex said. 'It was you who chickened out the other night, not me. I was ready enough to treat you as flesh and blood—'

'Oh yes – for a night – and then back to that hole in the ground.'

'All right. It was you who wanted to bargain, not me. I'm interested in digging for opals, I admit it. So what? Do you want me to prove *my love*' – even from this distance Frazer could hear the heavily sarcastic intonation in his voice – 'by dropping the opal bit after all my hard work, and trotting off like a good little dog with you? You wouldn't marry me anyhow, if it came to the point. Even if I asked you. Not even if I happened to strike it lucky here—'

'Strike it lucky!' Caryl was the sarcastic one now, and Frazer wished she couldn't hear. Caryl had been her friend at school and there was something disillusioning in finding the familiar image so distorted – by love, by jealousy. She couldn't get into her dress quickly enough to get away. 'That cattleman up at the homestead says there's nothing here – he should know.'

'Because he knows cattle? That's his subject – opals are Frazer's.'

'Frazer, Frazer, Frazer!' raged Caryl furiously, and Frazer covered her ears hard.

A minute later she uncovered them and there was silence. She buttoned her dress with fingers that shook, took her cassette and moved silently outside and away from the camp. Switched on some music, and gradually turned up the volume. She didn't know if they were fooled or even if they heard, but it made her feel better, and she tried to pretend to herself that she had heard nothing.

She was the one who got the tea that night – not baked beans, they didn't live on a diet of baked beans, whatever Jay Dexter thought – but mushroom omelette with salad. Caryl stayed in her tent and it was Rex who took her in a plate and brought it back again untouched.

'She's knocked it back.'

'She has a bad headache,' said Frazer quickly, 'I'll make some tea presently – that will do her good.'

'Oh, she's sulking,' said Rex. He piled another helping on top of the food that was to have been Caryl's and callously sat down to eat. 'Like all little rich girls, she's spoiled. Let her cool down in solitary confinement.'

Frazer didn't comment. Caryl wasn't spoiled – but she was in love, and she was having a rough time. In Frazer's view, she'd made a mistake in falling for Rex, but then, she supposed, one couldn't choose who one would fall in love with. She only wished she could convince Caryl that she had no reason to be jealous of *her*.

'How did it go this afternoon?' she asked, sitting well away from Rex, her plate on her knee, the glow of the small fire on her face. It could have been so lovely here, with the starry sky above and the soft night sounds all around – if only the company had been different.

'I didn't strike anything,' said Rex. 'Next thing will be to open another drive, I suppose. That would be easier than sinking another shaft – I'm not coming at that. How far do you reckon we should tunnel before we give up?'

They talked for a while, and later it was Rex who insisted on taking a mug of tea in to Caryl, plus a thick slice of bread and butter. When he emerged, he remarked, 'Money doesn't do pretty girls any good. Just because

Caryl happens to have been handed a pub on a plate, as it were, she thinks blokes like me that haven't got anything are going to run around her in circles.'

Frazer listened silently and thought a little sadly of Caryl's confidences at the very start of this venture – 'We just fell in love with each other,' she'd said. Now it looked like it was all going wrong, but there was nothing Frazer could do about it. They would have to sort out their own problems.

When she went to bed she dreamed of Jay Dexter – of his arms around her and his lips on hers, and then Rex had her by the shoulders and was dragging her into the shaft, and her father's voice was saying, 'We've got to find it, Princess – you and I together.'

In the morning, Caryl was up early, getting the breakfast and determinedly bright. Perhaps she had dreamed too – or else she had done some logical thinking. However hard it was to understand, she was in love with Rex, but she hadn't been playing her cards very well. Frazer was completely ignorant of how to win a man, but even she knew that Caryl had been going the wrong way about it. How do you learn? she wondered. Her eyes had strayed in the direction of the homestead, and she turned to Caryl about to say, 'By the way, any time we want a bath, we've been invited to use the bathroom at the homestead. I've been using my wiles on Dexter.' Yes, that would be a good thing to say – it would prove to Caryl that she wasn't interested in Rex, and—

But she didn't say it, because Rex appeared then. He came quietly up behind Caryl, put his arms around her and kissed her nuzzlingly on the side of the neck. Frazer turned away, embarrassed, to tend the fire.

Rex had already been up to the shaft, and as soon as breakfast was over, he went back. Caryl said brightly, 'Let's go up to the mine, Frazer. I feel fine today.'

Frazer thought quickly. Now was her chance to keep out of the way and let the other two consolidate what looked like a better relationship. She said lightly, 'You go, Caryl. I'll do the dishes. I might come up in an hour or so

– but I'm a bit tired of squatting about in that hole. I need a break.'

Caryl's green eyes looked at her warily, but she accepted the suggestion, and presently Frazer had the camp to herself.

Perhaps deep down she had known all the time what she was going to do that morning, though as she did the dishes and tidied up she didn't admit it to herself. On the surface of her mind she pretended that she would go up to the mine, rake over the mullock. You never knew – you might find something. Then she would come back and make something for lunch – cook a damper in the ashes the way her father used to do when she was a child. It was not till she was actually heading for her motorbike under the trees that she admitted to herself what she was up to. More than anything – more than looking for opals, more even than finding opals – she wanted – she wanted to see Jay Dexter.

Why? She hadn't the faintest idea. It was as though she had a fever – a sickness. It was akin to the opal fever that her father had had, that *she* had had.

She had put on clean jeans – light blue ones – and a creamy top, sleeveless, of soft silky cotton. Tan sandals, and no helmet, so that her tawny, gold-streaked hair fell softly and cleanly against her neck. What had he meant when he had said, 'Someone should teach you how to be a woman – before you learn the hard way'? She knew that she was already learning to be a woman, and she had an uneasy suspicion that somehow it was Jay Dexter who was teaching her, without being aware of it. She had been little more than a schoolgirl when first she came to Wandalilli. Now everything was changing. Her dreams had lost their crystal clarity, her friendship with Caryl had been damaged, and here she was, forgetting her mission, riding across the plain on her motorbike, her hair flying behind her, feeling the ground springy and alive after the rain. And looking for Jay Dexter.

And she had the feeling, just like the feeling her father used to have every time he sank a shaft, that he was going to bottom on opal this time – she had the feeling that she was going to find Jay Dexter.

She rode a long way – on and on, through gates that she opened, then closed meticulously behind her, through endless paddocks where cattle lumbered, and moved away startled however wide a berth she gave them in her efforts not to disturb the stock. Because you don't disturb stock that's not being mustered. Now, how did she know that? Had her mother talked to her about such things sometimes – when she was five or six years old? She couldn't remember ... She saw a great dark brown goanna – a perentie – about six feet long. It puffed out the skin under its slender neck and reared up on its powerful legs, staring at her angrily from its ancient stony eyes. The bike swerved and Frazer felt her heartbeats quicken with fright, but she rode on, knowing the creature was harmless if left alone.

Away ahead, a few flat-topped hills broke the monotony of the horizon, and then at last she could pick out men on horseback, working the cattle. She rode more slowly, quietened, sticking to the shelter of trees as much as she could, until she reached a stand of mulga where she dismounted and stood, her hand shading her eyes, watching the men and the cattle.

She found Jay Dexter remarkably quickly, as though her eyes were sharpened by – by what? By familiarity, she told herself quickly. She watched him with an odd absorption, deepened by the fact that he was unaware of her. It was as pleasureable as watching birds flying, or fish swimming, or clouds swarming across the sky, and it was strictly impersonal. Or so Frazer told herself. He rode superbly and he was completely taken up with what he was doing. She watched him ride alongside an aboriginal stockman, their horses neck and neck. He shouted instructions across to the other man and then he was way ahead, as though that red horse of his had wings. The cattle were being rounded up for some purpose she didn't know, and Jay Dexter was plainly the intelligence behind what every man did. Some of the mustered cattle were being kept in a mob, others were allowed to rush bellowing away, tossing their heads, and seeking the shelter of the scrub.

Dexter's broad-brimmed hat was pulled down low on his forehead, and his carriage was beautiful – if you counted a good stockman's carriage on his horse to be beautiful, and Frazer did.

'I didn't come out here to Wandalilli for this,' she reminded herself with sudden unease, and she wondered at herself for riding over the plains looking for Jay Dexter. What part had he played in her father's death? 'As soon as I've written this letter I'm going to ask them to take me to a doctor', her father had written. And they hadn't taken him for about two days. That was a fact. It wasn't conjecture, it was plain unalterable fact. So—

Suddenly, startled, she knew that she had been seen.

She turned her back swiftly on the men and the stock and the horses, got back on her motorbike, and was off through the mulga and over the thinly grassed plain. Her heart pounded. She rode crazily, regardless of tracks of any kind – racketing over potholes and clumps of stiff dry grass at a pace that was worse than reckless. And she knew that *he* was somewhere behind her on his red horse – riding like a demon, intent on catching her.

The sun was hot on her shoulder, her tawny hair flowed out behind her, and her shadow raced alongside. She swerved suddenly to avoid a stump – hit another – and went flying into the air over the bike to land hard on the ground, all the wind knocked out of her.

She lay there, quite still, half stunned.

In seconds, Jay was crouching on the ground beside her.

'Kate, are you all right? My God!'

She opened her eyes, widened them, looked up at him too winded to speak. Now he was on his knees, his arms were helping her to sit up, his dark eyes were luminous and intent. He was breathing fast and she could see his chest heaving, and she could see the sweat glistening on his brow. He was hatless now, and a lock of black hair fell forward, lustrous in the sun. Frazer couldn't get breath enough to tell him she was all right, she could only stare at him, and after a minute he pulled her to him and held her cradled against his body as if she were a child. Seconds went by, and gradually the pain in her chest eased, and her breath became more normal, though it still hurt.

'*Are* you all right, Kate?' he asked again, and she could feel the warmth of his breath on her hair.

'Yes – I hit something—'

'No wonder, the pace you were setting. What the devil possessed you? What were you escaping from?' He didn't ask, 'Did you know I was behind you?' but somehow she thought he knew the answer to that question.

She said, moving a little, 'My bike—'

'Your bike's all right,' he said tersely. 'It's you I'm concerned about. You should have had your helmet on. Do you want to kill yourself?'

'No,' she said painfully. He loosened his hold of her, his hands sliding down her arms, allowing her to turn slightly and look up into his face. It was a strange, disturbing moment as their eyes met. She felt a quick unpremeditated question rise in her heart. 'It wasn't you, was it? It was the Old Man.' A thought that came from nowhere and that she didn't voice.

He was frowning slightly. 'If you're going to pass out, tell me and I'll get you into the shade. You're as pale as death.'

'I'm all right,' she said. 'Just – winded.' She wondered when he would reprimand her for being in forbidden territory, but he didn't – not yet anyhow – and she felt his fingers gently caressing the smoothness of her bare, lightly tanned arm, while his eyes seemed almost absently to explore her face. 'Why did you ride after me?' she wondered. 'Why did I run away?' Maybe he knew – he was well ahead of her when it came to worldly knowledge. But not – not when it came to opal lore.

'What are you thinking? Something's amused you,' he said abruptly, and she realized she was smiling.

She shook her head confusedly. 'I was just thinking

about opals,' she said lamely.

His mouth curved sardonically, and his hands stayed still on her arms. 'Your grand passion,' he commented dryly. 'Well, it's something to know you're still thinking of opals at a time like this. If you'd broken your leg – or your neck – you might have had some rather different thoughts . . . D'you think you can stand up now?'

So he had had enough of holding her – and she had been lying back here as though— She cut off her thoughts and moved away from him quickly and got to her feet, feeling almost as wobbly as a new-born foal, but determined not to show it.

'I'm fine. You can forget all about me and go back to your cattle. I'm sorry to have troubled you – Mr. Dexter.' Their eyes had locked, but suddenly she couldn't keep it up. Her lashes came down and she stooped to brush some of the dust from her clean jeans.

'It was my fault,' he said unexpectedly. A pause and she had the feeling he was going to say something further to explain why it had been his fault and her heart began to hammer. Then with an upward twist to the corners of his mouth he said only, 'Don't forget to come up to the house for your bath – Kate.'

Banal, prosaic, even mocking.

She swallowed hard and turned away.

In another moment he was back in the saddle, looking down at her aloofly as she shakily made her way to her bike, righted it, got herself seated and the motor going. If you *must* do something, then somehow you do it, and in a matter of seconds she was off across the paddock, riding back to the camp as though nothing at all had happened. As if there were no pulse beating frantically, nervously, at her temples . . .

Back at the camp, there was no sign of Caryl or Rex. The bike had gone, and she assumed they had gone into town again. It was a relief to be alone, she felt shaken still, and it was not only because of her fall.

She buttered some bread, sliced up a couple of tomatoes, and opened a can of lemonade, and lunched in the shade of the trees. It struck her – quite wrongly, as she later discovered – as a good sign that Rex and Caryl had gone off together. They must have made up their quarrel and possibly Rex had compromised, and taken Caryl to town for some fun, since she had agreeably worked with him all morning. Optimistically, Frazer hoped they would all work together better after this.

She rested for some time in the shade, but at last stirred and, aware of a slight and unaccustomed feeling of distaste, got back into her dirty working clothes and went back to the shaft. She had been down dozens of mines in her young life, but she couldn't remember ever before having felt so reluctant. The pick and shovel were where Rex had thrown them, the floor was clear, the bucket empty. Rex had tossed out all the dirt he had displaced from the tunnel, and it was heaped on the ground at the top of the shaft. Frazer crouched in the tunnel and using the chisel end of the pick, drove it into the roof a few times. Soft opal dirt and nothing more. For how long could you go on working with fanatical, groundless hopes, down here? She felt a deep and fleeting sadness for her father and his dreams, and suddenly she threw down the pick, crawled out of the tunnel and climbed back up to the ground above. She moved up the slope and lay down on her back under the small twisted trees where Caryl used sometimes to sit. The earth was hard and rough, and she closed her eyes. Both her body and her mind felt bruised and broken. 'It's that fall I had,' she thought. 'It shook me up.' Her mind wandered wilfully back to those mad minutes this morning when she had careered across the plain with Dexter in pursuit. Why? she wondered again. He hadn't offered a word of explanation when he caught her – he hadn't abused her for trespassing where she was not wanted. But he had said that what had happened had been his fault.

What would he have said if she had asked about the Old Man – his father? 'Yes,' she imagined him saying, 'I was out on the run when Lee Madigan came to ask for a lift into town. The Old Man just didn't realize how serious it was.' Could it have happened like that? And where was the Old Man now? Frazer's eyelids lifted fractionally. She could see the grove of trees around the Wandalilli homestead. 'My father would have gone back again,' she thought. 'Yet even then—'

Suddenly her thoughts were intolerable and she jumped to her feet, wincing at the pain that shot down her back, and went down to the camp. She changed into her button-through dress and took her poverty pot from its hiding place in her pack. It was a long time since she had looked at the stones her father had given her before his death. The storm had interrupted her the last time, and now she badly wanted to see them – to reassure herself about something, or perhaps to revive a – passion ... She didn't really know.

The stones were wrapped in a scrap of silk, a patterned paisley that was part of a square her father had worn knotted round his throat under his shirt. The colours were faded and blurred now, but that scarf was part of Frazer's mental furniture, and to her the silk was her father's familiar scarf.

Two stones. Small enough and found on the opal fields by her father, brought forth from the dark earth when she was twelve years old. He had not given them to her to face, although even then she had been skilled at using the jeweller's lathe, and her small tapering fingers had rarely slipped. Her father had had these two stones cut by one of the experts who were generally to be found around the opal fields, and because of that, she knew he had hoped much from them. She remembered, too, her own breathless delight when she had seen them shining and beautiful.

'Dad! They're the best you've ever found! They're not big, but – they're perfect.' And she had watched the play of colour, the fascinating fiery pattern that flickered and burned as she turned the stones in her small hands.

Now they lay in her hand once again, and she saw with the old thrill the roll of red flame in the centre of the larger one, the night blue surround with its pricking of green-gold and emerald and orange. 'It's the Shining Flame,' she had said then, awed. 'And the other – couldn't we call it the Little Princess, Dad?' She remembered the hope in her heart as she said it, and how she had looked at him, wanting so badly to hear him say, Yes, this was the Princess he had longed to find. But he had shaken his head. These stones hadn't satisfied Lee Madigan. 'That's a name we'll save for a better stone than that, darling – a lot better.' She had hidden her disappointment, her wistful desire that they had found what they were searching for – that they had done it at last. Because he knew best.

But he hadn't sold the stones. She had only learned that when he had given them to her that day in Sydney. He had handed her this very marmite jar, watched her unscrew the lid carefully, with hands that shook a little, and unwrap the two stones from their scrap of silk. She had recognized them instantly and looked at him questioningly. Had he changed his mind? Or was it just that he couldn't bear to sell them?

'You keep them, darling,' he had said gruffly. 'Next time I see you, I promise I'll have something better – a real Princess.'

There had never been a real Princess.

Frazer, dreaming over the opals that now lay in her palm – the only ones she owned apart from the tiny stone she wore as a pendant – aware that the wide-eyed rapture of her childhood had gone for ever, still thought they were perfect. Jay Dexter might mock at her 'passion', but he didn't know that opals had been part of her life for ever.

'This is the best I could ever want,' she thought. This was the ultimate answer to her heart's longing for beauty and perfection. The pity was, Lee Madigan had not been satisfied.

And for some reason she knew that she could not possibly leave Wandalilli yet, content though she was with what she had here.

The others didn't come back to the camp till late that

night. Frazer woke to hear soft footsteps, and through the fabric of the tent she saw the faint gleam of torchlight. No voices – but she imagined them standing in the dark kissing, and she closed her eyes and turned on her side and assured herself once again that things were going to be better now Caryl and Rex had quarrelled and made it up.

When Rex appeared in the morning, dressed and ready for breakfast, she stared at him open-mouthed. He had had his hair cut and his beard shaved off, and though the newly uncovered skin looked pallid against the tan the rest of his face had recently acquired, the improvement in his appearance was remarkable. He no longer looked scruffy, and Frazer's instant reaction was a hopeful one. He had done it to please Caryl, he wasn't so bad after all.

She explained smilingly, 'You look beaut, Rex. I hardly knew you! I bet Caryl's thrilled.'

He put a hand to his shaven jaw and drawled out, with a strange look at her from his light-coloured eyes, 'I'm glad you approve. But as a matter of fact, Caryl's never seen what's underneath the whiskers.'

'What do you mean?'

He smiled slightly. 'She didn't come back with me last night. In fact, we parted company as soon as we reached Minning.'

Frazer stared, bewildered. 'But – but *why*? What do you mean?' she repeated. 'Isn't she – won't you – won't you go in and fetch her today?'

He shook his head. 'Not me.' He stooped to stir the billy of tea she had made, with a twig. 'We had a big row up at the mine yesterday morning, if you want to know.'

Frazer's heart sank. She moved the toe of her boot about in red earth that had turned to dust again. She had thought everything was going to be all right, and now Caryl had gone off and left her alone with Rex. It was incomprehensible. She bit her lip and asked futilely,

'What did you row about?'

His grey eyes were mocking. 'About opals – and you. Same old thing – Caryl's jealous. She complained I was more interested in opals and in you than in her. I didn't dispute it. So she got packed up – except for her boots and a few things – and I took her to Minning and there we parted company. She said I could have you and the mine all to myself for a few days and see how I liked it.' He poured himself a mug of tea, tipped in a lavish amount of sugar straight from the bag, and stirred it with a cucalyptus twig, while Frazer watched with a feeling of hopeless anger. 'I reckon she thinks you won't stay here alone with me.' He cast her an unreadable look and swallowed down a mouthful of the scalding tea. 'What are we having for breakfast – Kate?'

'Frazer,' she corrected him furiously. She felt she had received a blow on the diaphragm. She didn't know what action to take, what to do. She needed time to think, to assess this ridiculous and unreal situation. She didn't feel like eating anything, and neither did she feel like getting breakfast for Rex, as though she were – as though she were his woman. She said, 'Have what you like. I don't want anything – just a cup of tea.'

He grimaced. 'Now don't *you* turn temperamental, Frazer. And don't worry – Caryl will be back. She thinks I'm going to find I can't live without her, but for all practical purposes we're well rid of ser.'

'*We* are?' Frazer looked at him coldly. 'Caryl is my friend.'

'Was,' said Rex, setting down his mug and putting some more sticks on to the fire. 'Schoolgirl friendships don't always survive the conditions of adult life. I wouldn't waste any tears over Caryl if I were you. She's potch. You're—'

Frazer blocked her ears. She knew what he said even if she didn't hear it. 'You're opal.' She didn't want Rex talking to her in that way. It was – it was making a travesty of her dreams.

When she uncovered her ears, he asked, 'Where are the

eggs? Sure you won't have a couple? I was saying – you're a different proposition altogether. I haven't quite worked out yet what makes you tick. I'm not sure it's just opals. Or is it?' He made a sudden move towards her, a gleam in his eyes, and she stepped quickly away.

'Don't touch me,' she bit out furiously. 'Now Caryl's gone, you can go too. I don't want you around.'

He stopped where he was, within inches of her. His eyes sought for hers, and again she had that feeling of revulsion. He said, 'But I am around, Frazer. If you don't like my company, then you're the one who'll have to go. Because I'm not going. Not me. Not now, when I've done all the muscle work. I'm seeing this right through. If there's something here, then I want it. I don't own a hotel – I don't have an uncle who'll give me an easy job I'm not trained for.'

Frazer drew a sharp breath. She too stopped where she was, because she wasn't going to run away from him. If he touched her, then she would sock him one ... All the same, in her heart she was scared. If things became tough, who would come to her rescue? Jay Dexter was probably out on the run, the Old Man wasn't around any more – he had either retired to the coast or he had died. And up at the homestead there was only Dolly, and probably an handyman or two. Nobody who would be looking out for her interests. So exactly nobody would come to Frazer Madigan's defence if this man chose to get nasty. But it wouldn't happen – she was sure it wouldn't happen. Rex was more interested in finding himself a fortune in opals than in forcing himself on her.

An eternity seemed to have passed, and then he was the one who moved.

He picked up the frying pan and said coldly, 'I'm cooking eggs. If you want any, now's the time to speak.'

'I don't,' she said flatly, her voice calm. She sat down on one of the camp stools because her legs were suddenly shaky. She poured herself a mug of tea, hoping he wasn't watching and wouldn't see how her hand shook. Busy with the frying pan, the dripping, the eggs, he ignored her. She buttered herself a thick slice of bread and sat where she was, eating it slowly, watching him, saying nothing. She wasn't going to be bluffed into hiding in her tent. She was entitled to sit here eating whatever she chose to eat and doing whatever she chose to do. He fried himself three eggs, a couple of slices of bread as well, helped himself to salt and pepper and tomato sauce, and then ate quickly, ignoring her as she was ignoring him.

Finally he put down his knife and fork and looked across at her. She was sipping slowly, leisurely, her second mug of tea, prepared to show him her strength. He got up. 'Are you coming to the mine?'

'When I'm ready.'

He glanced back over his shoulder in the direction of the homestead, which looked a long way off to Frazer at this moment. Then he said, 'You haven't anything to complain about, have you?'

'Not a thing,' said Frazer steadily.

The flicker of a smile lit his unpleasantly light eyes. 'I wonder which one of us'd win if it came to blows – me or your lordly cattleman.'

Frazer didn't answer.

He moved and put a hand on her shoulder. 'Don't you worry, Frazer – you won't need to complain about me. I've got other things on my mind for the moment.'

Frazer shook off his hand. 'I'm not worrying. I can look after myself.'

There was a pause. Then he said softly, 'Oh no, you can't. How many pretty girls do you imagine have made just that remark and then found how wrong they were? Anyhow, let's forget personalities for a while, huh?'

'Why not?' Frazer marvelled at the steadiness of her voice. She stood up to indicate that she was going to clean up.

A few minutes later she heard him whistling as he strode off across the flat towards the mine.

'So what do I do now?' she asked herself several times during the morning. Rex had said Caryl didn't think she would stay there alone with him, and of course she didn't want to. Despite her boast, she wasn't all that sure that she could control him if it came to the point. But this had been *her* venture at the start, and she was determined to see it through. The thought of being intimidated by Rex was intolerable. She hadn't let Jay Dexter's opposition deter her, though that was a very different kettle of fish ...

Anyhow, because of the two of them, and perhaps because of one of them rather more than the other – she slurred over that thought rather quickly – she was going to stay at Wandalilli till she was ready to go.

By lunchtime she had made some sort of a decision. She would ride in to Minning, find Caryl, who was probably waiting there in the hope that Rex would come to his senses, have a good straight talk with her and persuade her to come back. It would be a start.

She prepared lunch for the two of them, in a perfectly civilized way, and as if everything were normal. There was salad with cold tinned meat, and she even put a can of beer to cool in a shady pool close to the river bank.

Rex looked at her sharp-eyed when he came down for lunch, and she found some satisfaction in his obvious surprise that she had got the food ready. He had a wash up, then sat down on one of the camp-stools and took the plate and the glass of beer she handed him.

'You didn't come up. Not interested in knowing whether I've found anything?'

'Have you?'

He shook his head. 'Not yet.'

Not yet. That was what they always said, thought Frazer cynically. Except the ones who were lucky. And when you'd been in the game for years, it didn't seem to matter if pretty often you had to say 'Not yet'. Because you always knew you'd find something sooner or later. Oh yes, the men who kept at it made a living. On the opal fields, of course. Not in an isolated, unproved place like this.

'I'll strike opal sooner or later,' said Rex with a confidence that Frazer found laughable. He added good-humouredly, 'You'll come up this afternoon, won't you?'

'No. I'm going in to Minning.'

His eyebrows rose in surprise. 'What for?'

'To bring Caryl back.'

He shrugged. 'You're wasting your time.'

Frazer didn't argue.

She tidied up before she went, then got into her light blue jeans and a matching denim jacket. Shoes instead of boots, and her crash helmet for safety's sake. She didn't much enjoy the long ride to town, because her back was bruised, but she just had to talk to Caryl. She would tell her, 'You don't need to worry there's anything between me and Rex, because there isn't. And looking for opals can be fun if you let yourself go. Just stay a few more days – it will please Rex as well as me. Just till—' Till what? Till Rex gave up? Or till Frazer came to her senses and gave up too? 'I'll play it by ear,' she thought confusedly, and wished that she and Caryl could giggle over it the way they used to giggle over scrapes at school. But it wasn't like that any more, and she had no idea what Caryl's attitude would be. Caryl wasn't any longer the girl she had known at school.

When she reached Minning she went straight to the motel, because that was the nicest place in town to stay, and Caryl would choose it instinctively. She discovered that Caryl had chosen it. She had stayed there the night, but this morning, the manager informed Frazer, she had left in a car for White Cliffs with a couple of girls she had met up with.

'They're going to spend a couple of days looking for opals,' Frazer was told. Her heart sank. She couldn't get Caryl to come back now. She thanked the motel manager and went back into the street, filled with a feeling of helpless frustration. There was nothing for it but to go back to Wandalilli and battle it out alone. And hope that Caryl would turn up in a few days' time. She hadn't taken many paces when someone took hold of her elbow from behind.

'Well, *Kate*!' said Jay Dexter, drawing level with her.

'I didn't expect to see you in town today. What are you after?'

She blinked hard and held back the words, 'I was looking for Caryl.' She told him instead, quickly, almost guiltily, and aware of the quickened beat of her heart, 'Just a few things I wanted to buy.'

'Shopping! I see. Well, how about joining me for a drink? After all, it's not often we meet socially, is it?'

She felt thoroughly disconcerted. Jay Dexter asking her to have a drink with him! She looked at him warily. He looked well groomed and extremely civilized in light fawn shirt and trousers, black shoes, a navy and light blue tie. And his dark eyes and that long flexible mouth were smiling at her. Something in Frazer collapsed. She had meant to refuse – to say she hadn't done her shopping yet, and that anyhow she didn't want to fraternize with him, but instead she said weakly, 'Well, all right. I *am* thirsty.'

He held her arm and they continued along the footpath together. There weren't many people about, for Minning was hardly a busy town. A few men stood under shop awnings yarning, young mothers pushed infants in strollers, followed by small children licking ice cream cones. The odd local business man crossed the street or stood inside a doorway. Several people nodded or smiled at Jay Dexter, and in a few minutes he was ushering her into the one and only respectable hotel. It was an attractive old building with a wide awning over the footpath, and a longer verandah with a wrought iron railing above. Inside, it appeared to have been fairly recently renovated, and there was a small courtyard draped about with Dutchman's pipe vine, where chairs and small tables with red and white checked cloths were set out.

'I think we'll settle for a spot of shade,' Jay said easily, his hand cupping Frazer's elbow. 'The sun's still hot and if you're thirsty you won't want to bask in it.' He chose a table and ordered drinks without consulting her, while she took a seat with unaccustomed nervousness. Then he sat down opposite her, and she was looking straight at him with a feeling of confusion in her mind. His dark eyes flicked over her almost curiously as he clasped his long-fingered hands on the table. Then he said disconcertingly, 'You're looking fetching today, Kate. But rather pale. You didn't do yourself any serious damage yesterday, I hope? – Just enough to keep you out of the mine.'

She felt herself flush. 'I bruised my back, that's all.'

'That's bad enough,' he said. 'You were lucky not to break any bones.'

'If I had,' she said rashly, 'I'm sure you'd have been able to set them for me, wouldn't you?'

He looked at her frowningly, slightly puzzled. 'Possibly. Though I'm not entirely sure you'd have trusted me to do so.'

'I might have had to,' said Frazer. She wasn't sure where all this was leading her, whether she was going to follow up with some reference to her father's accident with the pick or whether she wasn't. The arrival of their drinks at that moment decided her. She held her tongue, and watched as the waitress placed two glasses on the table – a long cold beer for Jay, and a long very pale pink drink for Frazer.

'It's not lolly water,' he said humorously, as she looked narrow-eyed at her glass. 'It's got just enough kick to make it interesting, but not enough to disqualify it as a thirst quencher. And I don't think even three glasses would have you half-way under the table, Kate, so get going and drink it down.'

She tasted it and found it agreeable, not too sweet, and icy cold, drank long and deep and half her drink was gone. Jay watched, leaning back, his glass in his hand.

'Better? Now, about you – and the real reason you're not working today. What's happened? Has your passion grown cold?'

Frazer blinked her violet eyes, feeling her hackles rise at the note of mockery in his voice.

'I have to take a break sometimes, don't I?'

'Yesterday morning, and now this afternoon,' he said thoughtfully. 'That's quite a break. You've had nearly

125

enough of messing round in the dirt, have you? You'll be off soon, for home and the fleshpots.'

Frazer stiffened. Of course, he didn't want her there on Wandalilli. He would be glad if she tossed it in and left. She told him firmly, perversely, 'No, I shan't. I don't give in as easily as that.'

'You're tough, are you, eh, Kate?' His eyes were quizzical, considering, and she felt a touch of unease. Tough. Aunt Helen's tiger – half wild, blunt, without artifice. And fourteen years old. But he was wrong. She wasn't tough. She wasn't like that . . .

He finished his beer, she finished her drink, and he signalled for the same again. She wanted to protest, to say she must be on her way, yet she didn't. And when it came to the point, what was her hurry?

'Your friends,' he pursued. 'They don't give in either?'

Frazer thought of Caryl, who wasn't even there any longer. How long could she keep that a secret from him? She said 'No,' then had to look away, to pretend to search for a handkerchief.

'You're lucky to have such friends,' he commented dryly.

She didn't know how she got through the next half hour or so, but it seemed to go quickly enough. Perhaps the pink drink and whatever was in it relaxed her. He talked a little about his cattle and the benefit he expected to reap from the storm, and then for some reason or other she was talking about boarding school, and telling him that she and Caryl had been friends there.

'And Rex – isn't that his name?' he asked casually. 'Where did you meet up with him?'

'Oh, Rex.' Frazer moved her glass and her forehead creased slightly. She didn't want to think about Rex – waiting back at the camp for her. The sun had gone well down now, and the sky was pale green with a few little teased out golden clouds floating high above. It was almost too cool to be sitting outside, except that the tiled floor still breathed out its stored heat from the day. The flowers on the vine looked luminous and large, like flowers on a stage set, and inside the hotel, lights had been lit, and shone soft and warm. Here, she was – safe.

Jay leaned across the table and as she played with her glass, he suddenly put his hand over hers. 'Don't fidget, Kate. You were going to tell me about Rex—'

She gathered her thoughts quickly. 'Rex – well, he's Caryl's friend. She met him after a boring sort of party, and he was – different. You know – not the kind of man her parents particularly liked, so anyhow—'

'So she brought him along to do some opal gouging, did she? Am I to take it then that your aunt and uncle are more tolerant than Caryl's parents – that the idea has their full approval? I seem to remember you told me near the start of our acquaintance that they knew all about where you were and who you were with. That they let you do pretty much as you please, no questions asked.'

She bit her lip. 'Why wouldn't they? I'm not a child.'

'No?'

'No.' His eyes were holding hers strangely, and she felt a little pulse moving visibly at her temples.

'Sometimes,' he remarked, and the concentration of his black eyes shifted briefly to her lips, 'sometimes you certainly behave like one. In fact, Kate, I've found you appallingly – even frighteningly naïve on odd occasions.'

The colour flowed into her cheeks and then receded as her mind flashed back over one or two incidents when she must have appeared definitely naïve – her wooden reception of his kiss – the time she had swum naked in the river – even yesterday when she had raced away from him so crazily on her motorbike. Still, why should she care what he thought of her? Of course she didn't ... He wasn't looking at her now, thank goodness. He had taken the makings from his pocket and was rolling a cigarette absorbedly, and as she watched those long strong brown fingers at their task, she thought again of him stitching up the wound in her father's foot. Always before she had thought of it as a rough-and-ready cruel sort of bushman's job. Now she caught herself thinking that Jay

Dexter would be competent, acknowledging that a man living in the outback as he did must quite often be called on to perform a service like that. It was strange to think that he had actually known her father, even though it had not been well. What had he thought of him? The familiar image of Lee Madigan rose before her in her mind's eye. A dreamy, shabby man who had spent the better part of his life on the opal fields, eternally hoping that one day he would make a big find. The father whom she had loved and trusted, yet who, to Aunt Helen, was both inexplicable and intolerable.

Now Frazer looked covertly at Jay Dexter and wondered what he had thought. And what he would think if he knew about her childhood. If he would condemn Lee Madigan or if he would understand and accept. With a little surge of resentment, she reminded herself that he hadn't respected him enough to take him to the doctor when he asked – not until it was too late and he was beyond helping altogether.

At that exact moment in her meditation Jay looked up and straight into her eyes, and she felt herself quickly draw a blind across her face. He said unexpectedly, and without even the trace of a smile, 'You'll have dinner with me, won't you, Kate? Here.'

Her instant impulse was to refuse, and then she thought of Rex, and she didn't want to get back to the camp and find him still around. For that reason and that reason only she said 'Yes'. And she realized later that in doing so, she had taken a first step from which there was no turning back. Because that evening, spent in Jay Dexter's company, was the beginning of the end of her faith in herself as Frazer Madigan, her father's mate. All that evening she was vaguely and uneasily aware of two personalities that chased each other like chimera through her mind. One was Frazer Madigan, the other was a personality created by Jay Dexter – that of Kate.

CHAPTER SEVEN

JAY lit his cigarette and blew smoke. He said as if in explanation, 'It's dark already. I don't like to think of you riding all that long way back on your own. I'll drive you home when we've eaten. I can put your bike in the back of the station wagon.'

So concerned on her behalf! Frazer wanted to feel sceptical, but couldn't quite manage it.

Before dinner she went to the cloakroom to wash up and comb her hair, and she looked at her reflection over the washbasin with an odd intensity. She wished for a moment that she had some make-up with her – that she had worn a dress – and her violet eyes looked back at her almost accusingly. She said beneath her breath, 'Well, at least it's better than going back to Rex—'

She met Jay in the hotel dining-room. He had secured a table and he rose to his feet as she crossed the room, her head held high. Her heart beat fast to see him there – Jay Dexter, whose name she had abhorred for so long. And now she had agreed mildly to eat with him in a hotel dining-room in Minning Minning.

There were very few other diners as they began their meal – a couple of solitary men who ate and read their newspapers, two middle-aged women, a couple with a small child. They had lamb chops with mashed potato and green peas, and followed it up with the only dessert available – jelly and custard. Jay's eyes met hers humorously over the sweet.

'This must remind you of boarding school fare, I'm afraid, Kate. I'm sorry I can't offer you anything more exotic.'

'I'm enjoying it,' she said without thinking, then flushed deeply at the amused expression on his face. She had found the food good. The peas had been fresh and the chops tender, and she had accepted the jelly and custard without giving it a thought. She hadn't a sophisticated palate, and she was quite unused to eating out, except during that short spell in Sydney with Aunt Helen.

'No criticism, then, Kate,' he mocked. 'And you're not pretending, are you?'

'Should I pretend?' she asked, uncomfortably defensive. 'I suppose you think I'm – appallingly naïve. But I wasn't brought up on caviar and champagne.'

He grimaced. 'I didn't suppose you were. It's not usual boarding school fare, and school's not far behind you.'

She said, floundering and hurt in some way, 'You do harp on school, don't you? I suppose – I suppose you think you're giving me a treat taking me out to dinner.'

'As a matter of fact, I hadn't thought of it quite that way,' he said, his lips curving in a wry smile. 'But when it comes to harping on the childhood theme – do you know something, Kate?' He leaned towards her, his dark eyes glinting. 'I wonder if you don't ask to be treated like a child.'

'I don't,' she said, stung.

'No?' He raised his brows cynically. 'Now and again, you practically demand it. And here's another thought – you're going to have to make up your mind about it all pretty soon. One minute you act like a sexless, prankish schoolgirl, and the next you're—' He stopped abruptly, pushed away his dessert plate, and felt in his pocket for tobacco and cigarette papers, his eyes no longer on hers. Frazer, hostile and on edge, thought he was looking for the most telling way of saying whatever uncomplimentary criticism of her he had in mind. She watched as he shifted his tobacco to his other hand, then finally put it back in his pocket again, unopened. He looked up and said almost casually, 'Because you can't expect it to go on for ever, Kate.'

'What?' she asked, at a sudden loss.

'My God!' he exclaimed, exasperated. 'That blankness – that lack of feminine intuition and subtlety! It's just not credible. Yet you don't do it just for effect, do you?'

'Do *what*?' Fury rose within her. She wished he would

say what he meant and say it clearly and unmistakably. 'Why don't you say what you mean?' she burst out accusingly. 'I don't know what you're talking about—'

'No, you don't, do you, Kate?' So let's forget all about it ... Meanwhile, how's the jelly and custard? Have you had enough?'

Yes, Frazer had had enough – and not only of jelly and custard.

'Right then, suppose we go into the lounge and have coffee and a liqueur.'

She pushed back her chair without answering, and as they crossed the dining-room together he put a hand under her elbow and remarked, with a quick glance across the room, 'Looks like a gaggle of teenagers heading for a holiday on the opal fields.' Frazer looked, and saw half a dozen girls in jeans and boots, giggling over the menu, and she wondered why she hadn't even heard them come in. 'That's where you should have gone, Kate – if you'd really wanted to fossick. You'd have had fun, and you'd have found something for sure. I haven't unearthed yet just what made you pick on Wandalilli for your excavations.'

'Shall I tell you?' she wondered, as they crossed the lobby. Now was her chance, for sure. She had him all to herself – she could tell him all he wanted to know, and she could ask him some very leading questions. But would she? She found herself turning from the thought with a little feeling of dread.

The lounge was completely deserted. It was a smallish dimly lit room with low leather chairs and round coffee tables that had coasters on them advertising various brands of beer.

'We've got it all to ourselves,' Jay drawled, and she had a new spasm of uncertainty. She wished she had said she didn't want coffee, but already the waitress had appeared and it was too late, and she reminded herself again that if she was back to the camp late enough, Rex might have gone to bed.

She sat well back in the deep leather chair, her face in

shadow, and as she sipped her coffee she watched Jay Dexter surreptitiously. He was the only man, apart from her father, with whom she had ever dined alone, and she knew that a lot of people – and they included Caryl and Rex and Dexter himself – would have laughed incredulously if they knew ... She started a little when he said, 'Well, Kate, you haven't explained yourself yet.' He had picked up the tiny-stemmed liqueur glass, but paused with it half-way to his lips, and before she could collect her wits he remarked irrelevantly, 'I've noticed you wear an opal pendant, by the way. How's that for a conversation starter?'

Frazer's violet eyes widened. It was, if he had only known it, a very good conversation starter. The very fact that he had noticed her pendant at some time or other startled her. Neither Rex nor Caryl had ever caught sight of it, she was sure, and it was tucked well inside her jacket now. She didn't wear it for show. She never had. She wore it for reasons that were both personal and sentimental. 'Opals mean good luck,' her father had always told her. 'For centuries, emperors and sultans, princes and sages – and lovely women, of course – have been wearing them. They bring strength and vitality to men, and they enhance and deepen a woman's charms, as well as protecting the eyesight ...' So since she was six, Frazer had worn her opal, found by her father, polished by her mother – a tiny, fire-strewn opal, diamond-shaped.

Her hand went briefly to her throat and her fingers touched the fine gold chain as she said huskily, 'Yes. It's – it's a good luck token. It protects the eyesight – though I suppose you'll think that's just a silly childish belief.' She sipped her liqueur and his eyebrows rose slightly.

He said seriously, 'Not at all, Kate. There's room in everyone's life for superstition and magic. Who gave you your good luck charm?'

'My father,' she said, her voice low. 'When I was very small.' He said nothing but waited for her to go on, and somehow, although she hadn't meant to, she did. 'It was one of the first opals he ever found. Out at White Cliffs.'

She raised her eyes and looked across at him searchingly, challengingly, and he looked back, his eyes narrowed.

'Then am I right when I conjecture you've possibly spent a year or two of your life on the opal fields? It would explain your undoubted, and otherwise rather mysterious, knowledge of the game.'

So he admitted she knew something! Frazer, mildly surprised, said, 'More than a year or two. The opal fields were my home till I was fourteen.'

'I see,' he said speculatively. 'Your father was an opal miner, was he?'

'Yes.' She had taken herself by surprise in telling him so easily what she had refused to tell Caryl or Rex, and now she was slightly on the defensive. This was where he would say something derogatory and belittling about men who earned their living gouging for opals – *family* men. The sort of thing Aunt Helen had said so often it made it impossible for Frazer to get on with her. Frazer was always ready to defend her father to the full. Lee Madigan had been able to support his family, and she had been happy with him – very happy – and so had her mother, even if Aunt Helen said not. Her father had told her, 'Francie was happy', and Frazer believed him.

But Jay Dexter said, 'Well, opal mining has been providing a living for plenty of men since the fields were opened in Australia. Your father must have done well enough at it – unless it was your uncle who paid for your schooling.'

'It was my father,' said Frazer proudly.

He nodded. 'And you've inherited some of his ardour – his passion.' His expression was curiously detached and thoughtful. 'Is it just the compulsion of the search that motivates you, I wonder, Kate? Or do you have a passion for the stone itself? I find it understandable enough for a girl to set her hopes on finding a beautiful opal. But you – you spend your days digging in that old deserted shaft on Wandalilli where nothing's ever been found. So it looks like we've come full circle, doesn't it? The old question – why?'

Frazer drew a deep breath. Jay Dexter was pressing her to tell him the thing that had been locked up inside her ever since she set foot on his property – the thing she had promised herself she would tell him one day – to his discomfort. And then she would be asking *him* to explain. It was strange how different reality was from anything you dreamed up or imagined for yourself. Even Jay Dexter. She had always seen him hard-faced, a man years older than he had proved to be, a man with a cruel mouth and an ugly voice. But the man who sat opposite her now, regarding her intently – he had a warm brown face and lean cheeks, a mouth that curved just slightly in a fascinating, almost sensual way; eyes that – eyes that revealed everything and nothing in their smouldering darkness . . .

She said with an effort, 'Yes, we're back where we came in. And you're right, I do want to find a beautiful opal. Not a lot, just one. Just' – she paused to swallow, then continued painfully – 'just the one my father was going to find, the one he promised he'd name for me, the one he *would* have found if – if he hadn't—' She stopped. Jay Dexter's look of detachment, of polite curiosity, if you could call it that, had changed somewhere along the line – subtly, disturbingly – to something else. To something quite different. Frazer didn't know what it was, nor why it should silence her, but it did, and her heavy lashes fell and her mouth trembled a little.

'Go on, Kate,' he said softly, and his voice was the very opposite of ugly. 'I'm listening.'

Frazer couldn't go on, she couldn't finish what she had begun to say. In the silence she was aware of a hurried secretive sound as of something counting out time rhythmically, rapidly. It was her own blood, and she listened as though it were some crazy countdown. When it reached zero, it would be time for her to say, 'I came to Wandalilli because I'm Frazer Madigan, Liam Madigan's daughter. Do you remember my father, Jay Dexter? You ought to – you must have his death on your conscience.' In her mind she heard it all tumbling out confusedly, the accusation she had made mentally a dozen times and more. There was sweat on the palms of her hands, and she looked not at him but at the table top. At her coffee cup standing empty, at the small stemmed liqueur glass with a few drops of syrupy liquid at the bottom. 'I am Frazer Madigan – you killed my father.' Oh, there were any number of ways of saying it, with or without elaboration. He would understand well enough, there was no doubt about that.

Her breast rose as she drew a deep breath. Hammer hammer hammer, went the pulse at her temples – maddening, insistent – and the silence beyond that hammering had become intolerable. Frazer pushed back the hair that had fallen across her golden cheek. It was time to speak. She raised her lashes and looked at him, and for no reason her whole body went limp, and her resolve collapsed and disappeared.

For no reason except the way he was looking at her, silent, thoughtful, motionless, the cigarette in his hand obviously forgotten, burning close to his fingertips.

Frazer knew that if she said what she had meant to say, it would be like getting a genie out of a bottle. Things would happen that she couldn't control – there would be terrible destruction. Destruction of what? Again, she didn't know. But as his eyes held hers, there was – there was a rose in her heart. A flowering, a bud, a beginning. And if she spoke, her words would be a sword that would slash the flower to pieces.

It was a mad – illogical – mental image. But all the same—

She moved to rise from her chair, saying huskily, unevenly, 'It's time I went back.'

He rose too, narrow-eyed, frowning faintly, glancing at his watch. 'If you must, Kate. Your friends will be wondering where you are.'

'Yes,' she said. She moved ahead of him towards the door. 'Thank you for the dinner, Mr. Dexter,' she said, in a voice that was not quite controlled.

'Jay,' he said from behind her. 'Can't you think of me

as Jay?'

No, she couldn't think of him as Jay. Not ever. She ignored his invitation and hurried out into the night. 'You needn't drive me back. I can manage on the bike.'

'I wouldn't think of allowing it. You'll come with me.' It was neither argument nor persuasion, yet she gave in without a word.

Beside him in the station wagon, she simply sat back and suspended thought, because there were too many things she didn't want to think about. Her own inexplicable behaviour – Jay Dexter – the fact that she was now on her own at the camp with Rex. Jay talked a little. He asked if Caryl shared her enthusiasm – and she had no idea what she answered or whether she answered at all. And he said that Rex was certainly putting his heart into the digging.

'You girls haven't been up to the house for a bath yet, Dolly tells me. Don't forget the offer's still open, Kate. A hot bath can do wonders for aching muscles. I thought you'd have come up yesterday after your fall, as a matter of fact.'

Yesterday. Was it only yesterday? The miles went by, the ghostly trunks of gum trees appeared and disappeared as the car lights swept over them. The moon threw a faint silver gauze over the unending plains and the low-topped hills on the horizon were no more than shadows. It was all beautiful and silent and impersonal – and very, very soothing.

It was pitch dark under the trees where the camp was when Jay finally braked to a quiet stop some distance away.

'There you are, Kate, safe and sound. The others must have turned in already.'

'Yes.' She knew a sense of unease as she thought of Rex, but overriding that thought was another. 'Kate,' he had said. 'Kate or Frazer,' she wondered. 'Who am I?' She opened the car door and slipped out. Jay got out to and handed out her motorbike.

'Thank you,' she said, hesitated over adding, 'Mr.

Dexter', and left it unsaid.

'It's been a pleasure,' he told her, and she thought he spoke dryly. There was nothing exciting about dining out with her! He stood near her in the faint moonlight. 'Don't overdo it tomorrow, will you, if your back's still sore. I might come down and see what you're up to.'

'Might you?' Her heart began to thud. She didn't want him to come down and discover she was alone with Rex, and she wished she could say, 'Don't come, keep away.' The darkness of his eyes was deepened by the shadowy night, and she couldn't read what was in them, yet she was sure that in a minute he was going to kiss her.

He moved – but it was away from her. He said, 'Good night, Kate,' and he didn't even touch her. He got back into the station wagon, and with a disconcerting and uncomfortable feeling of let-down, she began to push her bike across the flat towards the camp.

So he didn't want to kiss her. Well, that suited her. That was fine – that was one less thing to contend with. Head down, weary, she picked her way carefully, aware that if she didn't want to disturb Rex she must go quietly. Yet she was somehow unable to give her progress her full attention. She had been so sure he was going to kiss her – so ready in her mind to push him away. Because even if she hadn't been able to bring herself to accuse, the facts were still the same, and she could certainly manage a rebuff. That would be instinctive to Frazer Madigan!

She realized suddenly that she hadn't heard the sound of the car engine starting up again, and she stopped and turned her head slightly. He stood behind her, not ten feet away, a dark shadow. He said questioningly, 'Kate—?' – and her heart began a senseless dizzying clamouring. She wanted to say, 'I'm not Kate – I'm Frazer Madigan,' but she said nothing at all. And when he moved silently to her and put his arms around her and sought for her lips, she still uttered not a sound. But she turned her head quickly, deftly, aside, feeling her cheek brush against the soft cotton stuff of his shirt. His body had a tenseness, a hardness, a strength, that made her vaguely afraid, and there was an apprehensive hush in the darknes of the night that enfolded them. They stood motionless, locked together for she didn't know how many seconds. Her intuition told her that it was only due to some fierce effort of his will that he restrained himself from forcing her head around and his lips on hers – from forcing her to meet the challenge of his kiss.

Finally he moved fractionally, infinitesimally, slowly, and she discovered she had been released. He said, his voice still and level, 'Kate, you are as unsophisticated – as innocent of guile and pretence – when it comes to kissing as you are in your gastronomic tastes. I think you must be totally unaware that you are a – desirable young woman.'

She didn't answer, but she was trembling. He touched her arm briefly and went, and she moved on silently towards the tents. She didn't know why what he had said hurt so much ...

She left her bike under the trees, and before she went to bed, she looked inside Caryl's tent. Just to make sure. It was exactly as it had been this morning, and of course that was no surprise. When she reached her own tent, she had a creepy, inexplicable feeling that Rex had been in there. She flashed her torch around for a few seconds, but of course there was nothing to be seen, and finally she stripped off her clothes in the dark, and got into her bedding roll. She wished now that she had not bothered going in to Minning Minning. It had been a complete waste of time as far as Caryl was concerned, and it had been a bad mistake to spend so much time in Jay Dexter's company. It had disturbed her in many ways, and before she fell asleep she promised herself she wouldn't let it happen again.

In the morning, while she prepared breakfast for herself and Rex, and the galahs and cockatoos flew screaming from one tree top to another, Frazer kept her mind determinedly away from the subject of Jay Dexter. She thought instead about Caryl who, instead of staying cooling her heels in Minning while she waited for Rex to come to his senses (no doubt she saw it that way), had taken an opportunity that had come up and disappeared for a few days. Poor Caryl! Frazer rather thought she was going to come out of her affair with Rex with a bruised heart. She couldn't see a happy ending to it.

Rex appeared presently and sat down on one of the camp-stools, his shirt unbuttoned, because the sun was hot already – not with the burning heat of summer, but with early autumn's gentler heat. Frazer stared at him for a moment, not yet used to his new beardless look. Certainly it was an improvement!

He grinned at her, obviously conscious of the impression he had made. 'You didn't talk Caryl into coming back with you?'

Frazer said, 'No. Because she's left Minning. She's gone to White Cliffs with some people she met at the motel.'

If she had thought he might possibly be taken aback, she was wrong. He merely shrugged indifferently and began to eat his breakfast, and his indifference infuriated her. Caryl deserved better than that! 'I'm not worrying – she'll be back.'

'Not to *you*, I hope,' Frazer exclaimed. 'I wish she'd never met you! You've got no feelings at all, and she's—'

'She's out for thrills,' Rex interrupted, reaching for the salt and pepper. 'Girls like Caryl don't get serious about blokes like me – not unless they're really silly. And Caryl has her head screwed on the right way around. Now you – you've got a different set of values, Fraze – I could really fall for a girl like you.'

'I'm not flattered,' said Frazer coldly. 'I don't like you particularly, and I don't like you calling me Fraze, either.'

He grinned. 'Kate, then.' Her cheeks flamed and he added maliciously, 'Oh, sorry, I forgot. That's your boyfriend's pet name for you, isn't it? How did you get home last night, by the way? I didn't hear the motorbike.'

Frazer didn't bother telling him. She finished her

breakfast and began to clear up the dishes. Rex went up to the shaft, and she thought with a touch of resentment that that was where she should have been. She had come here, as she had told Jay Dexter last night, to find one opal.

Yet in her heart she knew that was not absolutely true any more. Her quest for the opal was no longer the clear and passionate compulsion it had been. The issue had become clouded, confused. She wondered with a sense of vague unease, as she spread her bedding roll to air in the sun, why she didn't pack it in and go. Instead, she was determined to stay here at Wandalilli – despite Rex, despite everything. Despite Jay Dexter. After all, in the beginning she had come here in spite of Jay Dexter.

'Anyhow, I'll have to stay now till Caryl comes back,' she told herself. Caryl was, however foolishly, in love with Rex, and she had left some of her things here, and she would most certainly turn up again one day – pretty soon.

It was a kind of compromise, though not a particularly satisfying one. She knew that some people would consider her decision to stay on alone with Rex was a rash one, but she was sure she could cope. It wasn't as if you could call her attitude to Rex an encouraging one, and surely that was protection enough! So when she had finished her work around the camp, she went up to the shaft, and discovered that Rex had finished picking over the exposed roof of the tunnel. He would now have to begin chopping away the table of opal dirt on which he had been standing to enable him to drive further in. Frazer, who knew how easily a stone could be missed in dirt knocked down from the roof, took it on herself to go through the pile of mullock he had thrown out of the shaft.

She continued this work through the afternoon, and by evening was thoroughly tired out. She caught herself glancing over at the homestead as finally she and Rex made their way back to the camp. Jay Dexter had not, after all, come to see how she was getting on, though he had half promised that he would. He had forgotten about her bruised back, and about her too, she supposed. His cattle were more important to him than she was. Well, that was to be expected, and under the circumstances it was a relief.

As she sluiced her face and arms in a basin of hot water in her tent, she thought with longing of the luxury of a hot bath, and of how it would ease her aching muscles. But pride forbade that she should go up to the homestead, and she had the shrinking feeling that if she did so, he would conclude that she was seeking him out. Besides, she had made a resolution which, if she were honest, she would admit she wasn't anywhere near keeping, that she was going to forget about him.

She and Rex ate by the light of the campfire. The sky above was velvet-dark and rich with stars that swung low and golden and scintillating. They hadn't much to say to each other, and after Frazer had washed the dishes she said good night and went to her tent. She looked forward to relaxing with the flap opened wide enough for her to see the stars reeling in the heavens before she fell asleep.

Her bedding roll was still warm and clean and fresh from its airing in the sun as she spread it out on the groundsheet, and she was completely taken by surprise when Rex's shadow blocked out the stars.

Frazer didn't even wait to see what he wanted. Instinctively, she lashed out at him with the first thing that came to hand – one of her boots which she snatched up from the floor and swung at him. It caught him a solid blow on the side of the face, and he staggered back, swearing. Frazer stood, her boot at the ready, waiting for him to recover. 'Frazer Madigan's not dead yet,' she thought wryly.

'You – you *bitch*!' she heard Rex mutter savagely. And then, his ardour quenched, and possibly disliking her as much as she disliked him, he turned and disappeared in the direction of his own tent. Frazer, breathing quickly, her pulses racing, stayed where she was. She had proved to him that she could look after herself! If he should

141

choose to come back, of course, she didn't know if she would win again, but she was sure he wouldn't come. She looked across the plain at the yellow lights that shone from the homestead. That was how close help was – but it seemed a very long way just now. And she wasn't running to Jay Dexter for help unless she absolutely had to – partly because she didn't want him to know she was there alone with Rex. Nor, perversely, would she run away to Minning Minning and admit to Rex that he had beaten her.

She got back into the clothes she had discarded and lay on her bedding fully dressed except for her boots, her eyes wide open in the darkness. Gradually she ceased to listen for stealthy footsteps, and listened instead to the night noises she knew so well – the moan of an owl, the distant drumming of an emu. And then she was asleep . . .

Next morning, the side of Rex's face was bruised and swollen and she wished for an instant that he still wore his concealing beard. Even his eye was slightly closed up, and Frazer looked at him with a feeling of sick revulsion. Because she had done that – she, Frazer Madigan. She said nothing about what had happened, and neither did he. They breakfasted, and later she joined him at the shaft. They scarcely exchanged a word, but she worked almost as hard as he did, and when he took a rest from digging out the opal dirt, she took a turn and he didn't protest or even comment. She was filthy with dirt and sweat by the end of the day, and she had never in her life been so physically weary. She knew that her father would never have let her work like that, but somehow she had felt she had to do it – to show Rex. Now she needed a bath and she was going to have one. She told herself that she didn't even need to see Jay Dexter. She knew where the bathroom was, and she already had his permission to use it.

'I'm going over to the homestead for a bath,' she told Rex briefly when they had eaten their evening meal and she had methodically washed the dishes and cleaned up – which he let her do without any assistance, despite the fact that she had worked at his side all day. His pallid grey eyes regarded her stonily.

'For a bath? Or to tell tales and ask for protection?' he said cynically. 'If that's your idea, I wouldn't, if I were you. I might decide to tell a few tales myself – ones that'd be guaranteed to turn your boy-friend right off you.' His eyes held hers unpleasantly, and she shivered. He put a hand to the discoloured side of his face. 'I could even cash in on this welt you fetched me last night, Frazer. You'd be surprised the story I could tell about that. You just wouldn't have a feather left to fly with.'

Frazer said with a coolness she didn't feel, 'Don't threaten me, Rex. I've told you, I'm going for a bath. I don't need anyone's protection – if I decide I can't look after myself I can always go and sleep in Minning, you know.'

'True enough,' he agreed. 'And if I didn't have a few other feelings about you. I could almost admire you for not going. Well, you're safe enough now. I don't want to collect another wallop. That's a very effective means of getting rid of suitors, by the way. I'd certainly like to know where you learned your manners. Not at that ladies' school you attended, that's for sure.'

'You're quite right,' said Frazer. Yet she hadn't learned such manners on the opal fields either, she reflected soberly, as she collected her towel and soap and toilet things. She hadn't *needed* such manners on the opal fields. She had learned them right here and now on the precincts of Wandalilli. She was quite a girl, was Frazer Madigan, she thought bitterly. She reached into her pack for her dress, then changed her mind, and slung black jeans and a heavy black cotton shirt into a plastic bag and went out to pick up her bike. She wished as she bumped over the plain in the direction of the homestead that she were going away from Rex and never coming back. As for the other man in her life – she smiled wryly at the phrase she had used in her thoughts – she would be wise to steer clear of him too. She seemed to lose all her old values – even her own identity – when she was with him. He had the power to turn her life into a series of receding fantasies because he was so solidly compelling himself.

She cut out her motor some distance before she reached the house, left her bike near a tree, and continued on foot. She didn't want to advertise her arrival. She opened the gate into the garden quietly, and keeping in the shadows, made her way around to the side verandah. She found a door open – the door of the bedroom where she had slept a century ago – and in a few moments she was in the bathroom, had locked the door and switched on the light.

There it all was, just as it had been on the night of the storm. The same, yet somehow different. There were bath salts there now, and there was a new cake of soap. Two enormous towels, one cherry blossom pink, the other pale leafy green. 'The pink for me, the green for Caryl, because of her red hair,' she thought, and she felt a strange spasm that Jay – it surely must have been Jay! – had catered so especially for Caryl's red hair.

She ran her bath – not too hot, but lavish when it came to water. After all, there had been rain, and she hadn't taken up the invitation before, so she hadn't been prodigal with the precious water supply. The bath salts made the water smell heavenly – she had only used bath salts once before, Aunt Helen's, as a kind of experiment – and in no time at all she was soaking luxuriously in the bath.

When at last she got out she rubbed herself down, dried her dripping hair, which she had washed, then draped herself in the heavenly soft pink towel. And with the scent of the bath salts and the matching fragrance of the soap all about her, she was suddenly looking at herself in the big mirror.

She blinked and stared. All day – in fact, ever since she had swiped at Rex with her heavy boot last night, she had been Frazer Madigan. But now she didn't see the person she had been.

It was a long time since she had stood before a mirror and really looked at herself. At the camp, she had only a small pocket mirror and she didn't often look in that. And here, the night of the storm, and the other day in the hotel at Minning – she hadn't really seen herself. Now, wrapped in the fragrant pink towel, she was confronted by someone who was almost a stranger. So what was different? True, her usually golden skin had acquired a deeper tan since she had been at Wandalilli, and there were streaks in her tawny hair that were verging on silver, bleached to paleness by the sun's rays. But there was something further – a darkness in the depth of her violet eyes, a questioning curve to her mouth, a wariness in the way she held her head.

Suddenly, with a shock that made her catch her breath, she knew what it was. She had thought Frazer Madigan was well and truly alive, but tonight she had caught herself out. Frazer Madigan had vanished. Here in the mirror she was Kate. *His* Kate, Jay Dexter's Kate. And she was staying on at Wandalilli not because of any opals but because – because she had fallen in love with him.

She stared at her reflection, stricken. That was why she looked so different. That was the meaning of the look way back in her eyes. They were the eyes of a woman who had fallen hopelessly, unknowingly, in love.

And he would laugh his head off if he knew.

The thought dropped into her consciousness like a stone, shattering with a confusion of ripples the new knowledge that floated on her mind like a bright reflection on water.

She turned from the mirror shivering as if she had a fever. She discarded the towel and reached shakily for her clothes. Her body was scented now, and it was strange to pull on the heavy black shirt, to zip up the black jeans. She recalled unexpectedly the blue and green dress *he* had loaned her the night of the storm as she combed out her tawny hair with an odd desperation. None of it mattered. She wouldn't be seeing him tonight – she mustn't! Oh God, to think she had fallen in love with him! When – and how – could it have happened? And what was she going to do about it?

She pulled on her blue and white sneakers and wondered why she was so reluctant to go back to the camp. She was not afraid of Rex since she had walloped him – he had as good as told her that he would be leaving her severely alone in the future. So—

She bundled up her soiled clothes and stuffed them into the plastic bag with her unused soap, her towel, and her face-flannel. She opened the door quietly, emerged from the bathroom and stood in the short passage listening. There was a light along there, and for a second she wondered if she would go out through the house instead of through the bedroom.

What on earth was she thinking of? Was she looking for trouble? Chagrined, she bit her lip and went through the dark bedroom.

She was half-way along the path when he came on to the verandah and said as casually as if he had been expecting her, 'Is that you, Kate? Come on to the verandah and have a cup of coffee before you go.'

Her heart stopped and then leaped. Kate. Why did it do things to her just to hear him call her Kate? She should be hating him instead of falling senselessly in love. She was as foolish as Caryl. And she had been mad, mad, mad, and unbelievably naïve to imagine she could come to Wandalilli to play out her father's dream without taking into account the absolute reality of Jay Dexter.

Because he was that sort of a man.

CHAPTER EIGHT

LIKE someone under a spell, she climbed the steps to where he stood, desperately conscious of her tough black jeans, the uncompromising aggressiveness of her black shirt. Underneath it all, she was Kate, and it made her heart faint to admit it. Her father had called her Frazer on the fields because it wasn't good to broadcast the fact that there was a growing girl-child around. She had called herself Frazer at school for sentimental reasons – and because she hadn't understood. To Uncle Frank and Aunt Helen she had been Cathleen, but that had never made any kind of sense. Cathleen was nobody. Now Kate – when Jay Dexter said it?

She felt his eyes rake over her as she joined him on the verandah, but she didn't dare to look back at him. Not yet. And she saw at once that there were three coffee cups set out on the cane table. Three? Her eyes widened. Had his sister come back? Was that why he had asked her up? Her heart plummeted. She dropped her plastic bag carelessly on the floor and walked over to take the chair he held for her, and he asked as she sat down, 'Where's your girl friend? Still in the bath?'

She felt herself crimson. The third cup was for Caryl – of course! She said, awkward at the lie by implication, 'Caryl didn't come.'

He tilted his black brows. 'Why not?'

She struggled with the truth and abandoned it as too unpalatable. It didn't sound good to admit she was alone with Rex. She said with a shrug, 'She's tired—'

'Too tired for a hot bath? I had the impression she didn't take much part in the really hard work. However, she and her friend may be glad to be alone for a bit,' he commented dryly.

'Maybe,' Frazer agreed in a murmur. He poured the coffee, sat down and passed the sugar, then he said, 'You smell of red roses, Kate. Very delectable.' And again his glance flitted over her, conjecturing, frowning.

She contrived a casual smile though her heart was pounding. Just to look at him unnerved her. 'I used the soap and bath salts in the bathroom,' she admitted, sipped the scalding coffee and found her eyes watering.

'Oh? Dolly must have put it there. She's taken a fancy to you. I daresay it's some stuff Barbara's left about. It's a scent that suits you, anyhow.'

She wished she had the self-confidence that could acknowledge a compliment – for surely it was that! – gracefully. But shyness kept her silent. Besides, red roses and tough black jeans – plus a schoolgirl who knew nothing about either kisses or good food! If it had been a compliment then there was a fair degree of mockery in it.

She found she couldn't keep her eyes off him as she drank her coffee. She was seeing him so differently tonight. Yet hadn't she always found his looks good – been aware of the power and strength of character in his face? Admired impersonally its bone structure, the vitality of his black hair, the richness of the tan of his skin? Tonight he wore a cream shirt of woven cotton, and his eyes were dark with a warm kind of darkness. He was utterly and completely different from the man she had had such bitter feelings of hatred for since her father's death that it was practically impossible to connect the two. It was as though she had dreamed the whole sequence, and she wished deep within her heart that she had – that she had met him in different circumstances, normally, as any girl might meet the man she was going to fall in love with.

They talked about the work at the shaft, of course.

'You haven't found anything yet, I conclude. If you had, you'd have been bursting with it – ready to confound me, knowing my ideas on the subject of your chances.'

She smiled warily and admitted that he was right, and knew that he was looking at her hands. She had soaked all the dirt off them in the bath, but her nails, despite the fact that she kept them scrupulously short, were damaged and definitely not pretty. So what? Had Frazer Madigan ever worried unduly over not having long and elegant nails?

'Of course,' he was saying considering, 'I'm well aware that all this tract of land is regarded as being opal-bearing country. It could even be there's another White Cliffs or Lightning Ridge on my cattle run – but the chances of finding it by sinking a single shaft are very slim.' He paused and looked across at her, asking her to confirm what he said. She thought stubbornly of her father's faith and he said with a touch of impatience, 'Well, admit it, Kate, admit it. Think of it – thousands of acres of land, all of it, *possibly* opal bearing. You know what the odds are – you've lived amongst opal miners. Fortunately for me, I'm interested in making my fortune out of what's above the ground – out of what I can see.'

Frazer listened yet didn't listen. She was caught up in looking at him, cautiously and unobtrusively from under her lashes and with a little less caution whenever his attention left her for a moment as he leaned forward to set down his cup, or to shift the packet of cigarettes that lay on the table.

'So,' he was saying, 'what do you say the likelihood is, with a patch here and a patch there – miles apart, and not all of it by any means worth finding.'

'He's been reading about it,' she reflected, a little surprised, and she told him obstinately, 'Some people can *sense* where to sink a shaft. They warm to opal—' Even as she said it, she knew she no longer really believed it. Lee Madigan had always talked to her like that when she was a child, and she had loved to listen, and she had thought there was something wonderfully exciting and extraordinary about her father.

'Now you don't really believe that, Kate, do you?' Jay said reasonably, reaching for the coffee jug. 'Have some more coffee? It's just not scientific, is it?' he concluded as he refilled her cup.

Of course it wasn't. And looking back, Frazer realized that mostly, no matter how colourfully he talked, her father had followed – not exactly rules, but logic. Sinking his shaft close to the latest find on a field, following the principle that a seam of opal runs along a line. That was how he had made his living. But following whims, feelings, especially when it came to *the* opal – where had that ever got him? She moved restlessly. She had no idea what had led him to prospect on Wandalilli, and she supposed she never would know. It was sadly disillusioning that they hadn't found anything in the shaft, and now – she just didn't want to talk about it to Jay Dexter. She said with a shrug, 'Oh well, there's always luck.'

'Luck's hardly the thing to depend on if you're serious,' he commented after a moment. He had finished his coffee and was now lighting a cigarette – a tailor-made – after offering her the packet. He sat back and looked at her through half-closed eyes. 'You know, I'd have sworn when you first came on to my property that you were after a story. Then it seemed as if all you were interested in was opals. Now, when you talk about luck – I just don't know. How about telling me about yourself tonight?' He paused and waited a second and then added encouragingly, 'Perhaps your uncle's pressing you for a story.'

Frazer bit her lip. 'You said there wasn't a story,' she said swiftly, agonized because now, she knew, she didn't want to hear. She looked at Jay Dexter and her heart despaired. 'You can't fall in love with a man who's as distant as that,' she warned herself. But hadn't he kissed her – held her in his arms? Why, she couldn't begin to guess, and until now she hadn't wanted it. Or not consciously. Probably he would never again take her in his arms. He was like Rex – he had tried her out, and she had rebuffed him as she had rebuffed Rex, but in a more civilized way. And because he was a more civilized man, he had accepted it, and so tonight he was prepared to sit here in the half dark on the verandah, drinking coffee and smoking and talking to her about – opal-bearing country, about her uncle, about anything at all so long as it wasn't really personal. It would have been exactly the same if Caryl had been here too, except that Caryl would have livened things up by trying to flirt with him. A thing that *she* couldn't do. She could only look at him and wonder at the fact that she had fallen in love with him.

He said slowly, 'I still say there's no story. For newspapers,' he added with strange emphasis, and looked at her with a question in his dark gaze, as if he expected something of her. But she didn't know what it was. She looked back at him and hesitated. All those things she had believed of him couldn't possibly be true. He didn't look in the least like a man with a guilty conscience, or even like a man who would deliberately hide the truth. The story of a man who died? 'I made a bad mistake,' she imagined the words. 'I thought this miner fellow had eaten something that had upset him. I gave him a cure Dolly always swears by and then – well, I'm a working man, and I hadn't asked him to come here. I just didn't get down to his camp to check up as soon as I should have.' Frazer closed her eyes, feeling sick. You couldn't be in love with a man whose brief relationship with the father you had loved had been like that.

While she looked for a way to change the subject, he found it for her, because he abruptly left the topic of the 'story' alone and began to talk about the herbage that was springing up on Wandalilli as a result of the thunderstorm.

Frazer breathed an inward sigh of relief. For a bad moment she had thought he might tell her whether she wanted to hear or not.

She said when she had calmed down, 'Wandalilli must have belonged to your father once? Has he retired to the coast like some station owners do? or—'

A slight frown creased his forehead and he leaned forward to ash his cigarette. 'My father was killed in an accident on the property. It was during a muster, and he shouldn't have been riding. At least,' he amended it, 'he shouldn't have been doing what he was attempting to do at his age. But he was bred to the land and he was proud, and' – with a wry grimace that had something of affection in it – 'he wanted to prove his virility. He was thrown by his horse and trampled by a scrub bull. He died in hospital.'

Frazer saw the bleak look of fateful acceptance on his face and she thought with a pang of anguish – 'It could happen to *him* – now, while he's young.' It could happen any time. She had seen him herself, riding at the muster with those wild stockmen of his – and he had ridden faster than any of them.

He was looking straight at her. 'Death. It's inevitable and often unacceptable. But we go on – and life is good, isn't it?' He smiled faintly and switched the topic again. 'What about you, Kate? What do you plan to make of your young life? I don't know how serious you are about journalism, and I'll admit I find your way of going about finding your one opal – I think you said that, didn't you? – more than a little irrational. So – are you just playing around till you marry?'

She felt herself flinch. 'I shan't ever get married.'

He said quizzically, 'No? You'll feel differently when you fall in love. An attractive girl like you should be able to pick and choose, you know.'

'Me?' she said, with a shock of surprise. She looked at him suspiciously, desperately aware of her tough, hardy clothes, her sunburned face bare of any make-up, her broken fingernails. Completely unconscious of the beauty of her darkly lashed violet eyes, the grace of her supple young body. 'In this get-up?' she mocked herself.

'What's that to do with it?' His eyes inspected her, and then he added deliberately, 'Don't forget I've seen you in other clothes, Kate – and without them too.'

She blushed scarlet, knowing he was referring to the day he had come upon her – no, sought her out – when she had swum in the river. Though in all fairness, he could hardly have known she was bathing stark naked . . .

'You're attractive,' he repeated. 'More attractive then you know.'

She was struck by a sudden doubt. Was he – was he trying to boost her ego for some reason of his own? Was he – she flinched at the thought – preparing the ground for another attempt at persuading her to succumb to his charms? She hoped not – because she didn't know now how she'd react. She was thinking somewhere at the back of her mind, too, about her dreams, in what seemed another life, of meeting a man who would share her fever for opals. That had been the kind of man she saw herself falling in love with. And now she'd met a man who did just that – Rex – he was the last man on earth she would ever want to marry. Once, she'd have said Jay Dexter held that position. Now it was drastically untrue. And it hurt all the more that he was amusing himself flattering her – the schoolgirl; possibly even seeing himself as her instructor in the esoteric lore of how to be a woman. 'Someone should teach you how to be a woman, Kate, before you learn the hard way.' Through Rex's instruction, for instance? Well, she had taken care of that.

So now she'd better go while she was still in one piece. Her chair grated on the floorboards as she pushed it back. 'I'll go now. I didn't mean to come and impose on you. I didn't expect you to turn on coffee.'

'Don't be in such a hurry,' he protested. 'I've enjoyed your company, and I hope you've enjoyed mine a little, too.'

She had, of course – in a tense, mad, febrile way. Any girl, she supposed, got pleasure from time spent in the company of the man she had fallen in love with. There was pleasure in merely looking at him, in listening to his voice, in marvelling about love – Her case of course was different, because it was so impossible. Besides, she didn't trust her own feelings yet. She didn't trust him, either. She suspected him of manoeuvring her somehow, of playing on reactions she didn't understand. Maybe he was even somehow persuading her into falling in love with him. It was an uneasy thought.

'It's been very nice,' she said ridiculously, standing by the table, her eyes lowered to the level of his chest. He had got up too, despite his protest that she mustn't hurry.

'Well, that's a change,' he said, dryly amused. 'I don't claim to be a particularly sensitive man – I spend more of my time amongst cattle than I do with women – but I've had the feeling during our short relationship that you more or less hated me, for some obscure reasons of your own. I'd like to put it to you that where there's more knowledge, there's often a better understanding. Do you agree?'

Frazer said 'Yes.' She'd have said yes whether she agreed or not, because by now she felt a quite compelling urge to escape – to run away back to the safety of the camp – the irony of it! – where Rex and Rex alone was waiting for her. But with a billy of tea this time, she rather thought, instead of lust. She turned determinedly and stooped for her plastic bag on the floor at the top of the steps.

He reached for it casually. 'Here, I'll take that. I'll walk with you to wherever you've left your bike.'

'Don't bother,' she said in a panic. 'It's just down under the trees.'

'It's a lovely night. It will be no punishment.' He went down the steps with her, and added disconcertingly, 'Yes, red roses become you, Kate.'

They walked in silence through the garden, and he held the gate open for her. 'I wonder why you didn't ride up to the house? Did you want to hide from me? Never mind – it's an excuse to walk you part way home.' She supposed he meant it all humorously, but she didn't feel terribly amused. She had the uneasy suspicion he was treating her like a child. Well, maybe that was safe enough, but she didn't like it just the same.

She changed her mind about his tactics when they reached the shadows where her bike gleamed faintly beneath the trees, and he set down her bag and turned, his body close to hers.

'You clammed up the other night, Kate. You played hard to get – like a girl who's never been kissed – or never been kissed in the right way.' His hands were on her shoulders now, so firmly that she couldn't twist away if she had wanted to. And of course she didn't want to. 'I promise faithfully I shan't hurt you.' She could feel the warmth of his breath on her forehead as he murmured on, 'I don't know exactly what kind of a hang-up you've got, but relax – trust me—' He drew her deliberately against him, and she turned her face up to his, wanting more than anything in life to feel his lips against hers, to have him crush her body close – close – to have him love her, love her—

She stood quivering yet passive while his hands rested firmly on the soft flesh of her arms, and he waited, giving her a chance to say No – to move away, to escape, to say Let me alone. But she didn't move. Her pulses hammered as she waited too, and then he pulled her closer and kissed her long and deeply until she was completely lost.

When at last he paused to draw breath and to move a little so that he could look down into her face, she was trembling wanting to believe he felt as she did, knowing that in any case it was impossible, that she was betraying all the ideals and beliefs that had made her what she was. Then out of the corner of her eye she saw a soft patch of that green grass that the rains had created, and she imagined him drawing her down there and—

Her voice was little more than a whisper when she said, 'Don't get the idea I'm one of your liberated girls, Jay Dexter – like that girl whose clothes you had me – tarted up in the other night.' It was strange exquisite and torturing relief to say it, and to feel the old mistrust taking over again – the old hatred. She felt his fingers tense on her arms, and then he said softly too, but harshly,

'What the hell are you talking about, Kate?'

'You know what I'm talking about.' She said it aloud. 'And don't try to tell me it was your sister's dress. I don't know what's happened to the girl it belonged to since she succumbed to your – your sympathy and charm, but I suppose she soon woke up to how little you cared—'

'*Be quiet,*' he said through his teeth. He let her go and moved to stand three feet away from her. 'I don't know how your mind works, but it's certainly a suspicious mind. So listen – my sister brought that dress back from Indonesia at my request. I wanted a gift for the girl I happened to be interested in at the time. But by the time Barbara was back from her holiday, the affair was ended. That's the story. So no one's ever worn that dress but you,

Kate, and no one will ever wear it but you. You looked very beautiful in it – a barefoot princess.' She blanched at the phrase, and she had no idea whether he was making up the whole tale or whether it really was true. He said, 'I'll make you a gift of it when you—'

'When I leave here,' she finished for him almost violently. She stared at him through the darkness, trying to see his face, and she saw the line of his mouth tighten and his jaw tense.

'It's on your mind, isn't it, what I said to you that morning at the camp. You think I'm a man who thrives on brief affairs, who takes love lightly. Well, I can't deny my own past, but look, Kate, I'll make you a promise. When you do leave Wandalilli and go back home to Mingari, I'll be along. It won't be the last we'll see of each other by any means. I'll want to learn to know you better—'

Frazer's lip curled. A promise! Give in to me now, and maybe next year I'll marry you. Wasn't that what he implied? She didn't have any experience of men, but still, she wasn't silly enough to fall for that. She told him tightly, 'Don't bother making any spurious promises, Mr. Dexter. I don't expect to see you again once I get off your property.'

There was a pause, and she wished she could see his face clearly yet was glad she couldn't. When she had hit out at Rex, she had felt justified, unrepentant. Hitting out at Jay was different. She knew she had to forget him, and she thought, 'Oh God, why do I have to know too much about him?' Why couldn't it have been otherwise? Why couldn't she have been able to hope—

She saw his mouth twist wryly and heard him draw an exasperated breath. 'Well, it's all in the future, isn't it? You haven't gone yet. You're well and truly dug in at Wandalilli. And I think you're as tired as death. We'd better say good night.'

He looked across his shoulder and Frazer looked too, and she could see glimmering over there across the dark invisibility of the plain the faint red glow of a fire.

She said, 'Yes. Rex — they're waiting up for me.'

Again his lips twisted. 'Waiting up. Well, you've come to no harm, have you? Do they think me such a dangerous character? Is that why your girl friend didn't come up for a bath? I'll begin to wonder what terrible tales you've been telling about me, Kate.'

'I haven't—' she began, then stopped. She didn't know if he was making fun of her. She didn't know if he cared even the slightest little bit when she'd said she didn't expect to see him again.

She got on her bike and started it up and rode off unsteadily into the dark. Despite the bath, her muscles were aching — and so was her heart. Her mind was utter confusion. She didn't know what she had done — what she had refused — what he had offered. She had ventured way out of her depth and now she was regretting it.

Sure enough, Rex had made a billy of tea and was sitting lazily by the fire. He said, 'So you've come back, Fraze. I began to wonder if you'd got yourself invited for the night. Was he sympathetic when you told him I was such an unbridled beast? Has he provided you with a rifle to defend your honour? Or did you discover he doesn't want to know? It's not every man that has an eye for such a rough little customer as you.'

'Yak yak yak,' said Frazer — and it was certainly Frazer speaking, not Kate. She slung her bag inside her tent and came to sit on one of the camp stools. 'I didn't find you worth mentioning.'

He looked at her in the firelight and he was grinning a little.

'Never mind, Frazer. You smell good. Want any tea?' She said, 'No,' and he got up and threw the contents of the billy on the red ashes of the fire. 'Now you're safely home — I'll be a gentleman and put it that way, anyhow — I'm going to have some shut-eye, and I'd advise you to do the same. See you in the morning.' He gave her a slap on the back that was too hard to be friendly as he passed by her, and for one reason and another Frazer felt that life had reached a very low ebb.

She was up early next morning, but Rex was even earlier. When she emerged from her tent he was already at work on the slope, with pick and shovel.

It was barely light, the stars still hung pale and glimmering, green-gold in a sky that changed colour as she watched. She was glad Rex had gone. She had always loved to be about at sun-up, and she had the feeling that this might be one of the last sunrises she would ever see at Wandalilli. She stood just clear of the trees and watched as a few distant clouds began to brush high across the heavens in sweeps of apricot pink, that deepened and dazzled as the sky turned turquoise. On the horizon, the clouds drifted into gold, and beneath them the sun was emerging from the grey shadow of night that still hung over the edge of the world. A sun so red, so clear cut – this was the time when you could really look at it and see the source of light and warmth on which your life depended. See it, and marvel . . . It was still shadowy down here on the plain, but in the upper reaches of the air, the larger birds were rising to float and ride on soft high currents in the red light of the sun. Frazer watched thcm as they glided, wings steady, silhouettes now red, now black, as they turned in the early morning light, rejoicing in their own way in the newness of the day. And it was strange, but mixed up with it all at the back of her mind was the thought of Jay Dexter, the man she both loved and hated.

She became aware that someone was watching with her, and she turned her head to find with a strange shock Jay Dexter himself – perhaps twenty feet away, and silent, motionless as she was herself. Why? she wondered, why had he come here now – so early?

He turned almost at the same moment as she did, then came towards her across the ground where the new grass had sprung.

'Good morning, Kate. You're up early. I see your boy-friend's at work already.' His dark eyes, glinting fiery in the red light, flicked over her, looking for what she didn't know.

'Caryl's boy-friend,' she corrected him automatically,

aware that she had flushed under his regard.

He tilted his brows. 'How's Caryl this morning? Not up and about yet?'

Frazer's flush deepened, and she couldn't meet his eyes any longer. She had a nervy jumpy feeling that in a moment he would go and call out to Caryl – discover that she wasn't there – and guess— And to ensure that that didn't happen, her mind tricked her into saying with a jerky brightness, 'Caryl's – Caryl's gone into town for shopping.'

She looked at him quickly, smiled, and moved to the box where they kept their stores. She took out a plastic bowl, a fork and six eggs, and set them on the top of the box. She began breaking the eggs carefully into the bowl. She hardly knew what she was doing, and she saw neither bowl nor eggs very clearly. Her mind was taken up with Jay, who was moving about somewhere out of sight, doing what she didn't know. She wished futilely that she hadn't lied to him, but she had – and she had lied by more than mere implication last night, too, so it was well and truly done now. It had somehow seemed important that he shouldn't know she was on her own with Rex, and she wished he hadn't come to the camp so early in the morning.

'How long's she been gone?' he shot out suddenly from behind her.

She jumped visibly and looked up from the bowl. He stood, hands on hips, glaring at her – his brows drawn, that black lock of hair falling in a dark wave across his forehead, his mouth very straight and just the slightest bit ugly. There was anger visible in his eyes, and as her gaze slipped away from his guiltily, she saw that his knuckles were white.

'Well?' he rapped out.

The blood left her face and she could feel the hair at the back of her neck prickle. She said idiotically, making matters worse instead of better, 'I – I don't know what time she left.'

He moved closer to her. His jaw tightened and the ugly line of his mouth was accentuated.

'Kate, we're two adults. You've been lying to me. Caryl's gone, hasn't she? I've looked in her tent and I know damn well she hasn't gone shopping. She wouldn't go at this hour, besides which there are still two motorbikes under the trees. She hasn't been around for days – has she?'

'Well, if you *know*,' said Frazer furiously, hating him for catching her out in such a stupid lie – knowing what interpretation he could put on it, 'why do you ask?'

'Because I don't know. Because I'm guessing. I hadn't noticed her about lately, but I'd supposed she was doing her usual stunt of avoiding the hard work – swimming in the river, maybe, or reading in her tent. I'd noticed too, by the way, that your boy-friend's had a shave and a general clean-up.'

'You know a lot, don't you?' Frazer flared. 'You haven't even been near the camp for days. Have you been spying on us all the time?'

He looked at her levelly. 'If you choose to call it that. I'd thought of it as keeping an eye on you, in case you should ever need my help. All the same – despite my *spying* I seem to have missed out on a very crucial move, don't I? And you certainly didn't keep me up to date. It makes me wonder what else I've missed.'

She crimsoned at his implication but flung back, 'We'd never need – or want – your help. And I'd never expect you to offer it – never. Not if I was dying. Not if—'

He closed his eyes momentarily. 'Be your age, Kate.'

She had set down the basin because her hands were shaking, and now began a frantic search for the frying pan.

'I haven't been all that bad,' he continued. 'In fact, one way and another I thought I was being quite reasonably helpful, under the circumstances.' He took two longer paces, reached down, then held out the frying pan to her. 'Is this what you're looking for?'

She almost snatched it from him. 'Letting me use your bathroom,' she gibed. She had discovered with bitter relief that she could hate him after all, in fact she thought she must have been mentally aberrated when she had imagined herself in love with him. 'I suppose I'll have to do without a bath after this. Well, I don't care, because — because—'

He snapped out, 'If you want to take a bath, you can use my bathroom. I don't give a favour and then withdraw it. You're exactly the same girl now as you were when I granted it. Exactly.'

His tone left her in no doubt as to what sort of a girl he thought she was, and she simply stood and listened while he went on unrelentingly. 'So what's happened now? Let's have it — let's have the truth. Have you swiped your girl friend's man?'

'No!' she said hotly. She faced him aggressively, and his eyes, black and harsh, looked her over with a deliberate cynicism. She tried not to imagine what he was thinking as his eyes raked her over. Frazer Madigan in working gear — boots, dirty jeans, rough-dried shirt. Had he ever kissed her? Had she ever wanted him to? Now he was probably thinking she was a fit mate for Rex Byfield, and she squirmed under his regard.

He took out cigarettes and lit one and she was pleased to notice that his hands were far from steady too. He looked at her still, and the flame of the match lent his eyes a threatening red glow.

'I'd like to know how that mind of yours works. You're the most prickly, mixed-up girl it's ever been my lot to deal with.'

'And I suppose you've dealt with a lot of girls in your time,' Frazer put in smartly.

He drew on the cigarette and looked at her through the haze of smoke, an odd expression on his face. 'That is one of the few adult remarks you've ever made to me, Kate,' he said calculatingly.

Frazer flinched, but she managed, 'I couldn't care less. And anyhow, I do happen to be an adult.' She scooped up a spoonful of dripping and put it in the pan, then set the pan on the fire.

'I'm beginning to believe you,' he said dryly.

She felt ready now to blurt out all the accusations that had been festering in her mind since first she hit Wanda-lilli, and that she had been – yes, too bemused to bring to the light before. He had fooled her right from the start, and she knew it now. Not any more though.

But before she had quite gathered herself together, Rex came strolling back to camp, sleeves rolled up, hands covered in dirt, sweat already glistening on his forehead. And his eyes – those strange hard eyes – shining most peculiarly as with a fever.

'Well, hello,' he remarked chattily. 'Visitors so early! Aren't we lucky? Hey, Fraze, the fat's about to burn—'

He and Frazer moved at the same time towards the fire, almost colliding as they both reached the pan. Jay Dexter, his eyes narrowed, his mouth grim, turned on his heel and walked away beneath the trees, and Frazer watched as he swung himself up on to the red horse and galloped away. 'Good,' she thought. 'If you'd stayed any longer you'd have been really sorry.'

'What's got into him?' Rex marvelled. 'Do I get the feeling that he hates my guts for some reason? Or did I interrupt something?'

'Just an early morning chat,' snapped Frazer. Her heart was dying within her as her temper cooled, and she would have given everything she possessed to be alone to weep, to let the tears that were stinging her eyes so bitterly fall. Everything was so hideous, so out of perspective, so untrue. The things that Jay believed of her – even the things she had said to him?

Rex was pacing about, and now he took the water-bottle and poured water into a wash bowl. He lathered his hands and splashed his face, then reached into his tent for a towel.

Frazer tipped the eggs into the pan and was stirring them blindly, her eyes swimming in tears, when he came up behind her and put his arms around her waist and squeezed her. He said, very quietly,

'Frazer, I've struck a seam. I'm on to opal. We're in the big time.'

CHAPTER NINE

FRAZER felt her heart stop and then begin a mad racing – in the old way, the way it had behaved when her father had said much the same thing to her. Then, she would have turned around and flung her arms around her father's neck, and they'd have done a soundless and ecstatic jig wherever they were. Now, she said coolly, 'I don't believe it.'

'You will when you see,' he said. 'You're a cool customer, aren't you? Don't you know what this could mean? Aren't you excited? Most girls would be going mad – racing up to see—'

'In the middle of scrambling eggs?' Frazer said dryly. 'Where's your plate?' The truth was, she didn't know how to act. She didn't even know how she felt. She had too many other things on her mind ... She sat down on a camp-stool and helped herself to salt and pepper, bit into a piece of bread, and tried to follow reasonably the visions that floated through her mind, and that all seemed to be overshadowed by the image of Jay Dexter's face as it had looked just now when he caught her out lying.

The consummation of her father's dream – the fiery palaces, the potch that might lead to the One and Only Stone ... So what? questioned some newly cynical part of her mind. What's a stone, after all? Particularly when on another camp-stool not four feet away, Rex Byfield was sitting, thinking too of opals, exulting in his find, his excitement all too plain to see. In a strange way, none of it seemed to have anything to do with Frazer.

A couple of minutes later Rex put aside his plate and took her by the arm. 'Come and see, Frazer. Come and confirm that we've found what you swore was there.'

She had never sworn anything was there. And although she had been confident once, that seemed an immeasurably long time ago, because in between times, something had happened to her that was a lot more dramatic than finding opals.

Somehow unwillingly, she went with him across the flat and up to the low ridge where the mine was, red and pink earth piled around. He had struck a seam all right. He had begun to gouge out of the earth hard, flat stones that had been hidden in the dark for centuries and centuries. What was the secret hidden in those stones she didn't yet know, but again her pulses were racing.

'Well?' he said, with a cocksure look.

She shook her head. 'I don't know,' she said perversely. She stooped and picked up a couple of stones, and at once her heart contracted as she saw a pinpoint of fire shining out from the dirt-encrusted grey potch. 'My fa—' She stopped and started again. 'It's potch, but there's colour in it. And that doesn't always lead to precious opal, by any means.'

'It will this time,' he said with a rough careless confidence. The glimmer of a smile lit his eyes. 'Down there in the tunnel – I saw all these little fires! It was incredible! It was what you promised—'

'I didn't promise,' said Frazer with faint impatience. 'You can never promise.'

Rex had jumped down into the mine, and seizing the pick began to gouge carefully away at the roof of the tunnel, and she heard the faint glassy chink as the chisel point struck softly against another stone.

'It's a seam,' said Rex triumphantly. 'There's no mistake.' He got to work with his fingers and in another minute tossed a stone up to Frazer, then emerged himself to stand looking at her expectantly.

Frazer smoothed off some of the dirt and turned the stone around with careful fingers. She said rationally, 'There's nothing to get excited about yet. A little bit of colour—' She looked up at him and went on, unable to help her own honesty. 'You'll have to work carefully now, Rex – the stones may be close together. You ought to use a pocket knife instead of the pick. And I'll – I'll look through all the dirt you knock down from the roof.'

'You do that, Fraze,' he agreed. His steely eyes were bright as the fire in the potch. He believed and nothing would make him disbelieve, and of course, as Frazer well knew, once you had found colour you had a very fair chance of getting on to precious opal, where even a handful could be worth a packet. Yet curiously, somewhere deep down, she couldn't accept that Rex might find opal. She just didn't believe that he would. Not here. And if he didn't find it, then Frazer Madigan wouldn't either . . .

As she went up to the shaft with him after lunch, she wondered if Jay Dexter would be along, and what he would have to say about their find. More still, she wondered what conclusions further thought might have made him reach about herself and Rex being here alone.

'I wish Caryl would come back,' she mused aloud.

'Caryl? Oh, to hell with Caryl,' said Rex offhandedly. 'Who wants her around, making trouble?' His light grey eyes looked at her speculatively. 'You and I make a good team, Frazer. Just don't hang on to the idea that I ever promised Caryl anything. She was the one who picked *me* up, believe me – and girls who play that kind of game deserve whatever they get. I only came along because I don't believe in passing up any kind of a lead. Well, I was right this time!' He threw up his hands and laughed suddenly. 'Caesarina! Christopher Columbus! I can't believe what's happened yet!'

Frazer raised her eyebrows. They had reached the shaft and as he sprang down she said dampeningly, 'Nothing's happened. If you'd been connected with opal mining as long as—' She stopped and bit her lip as she stared up at her, his eyes narrowing. 'It's all a gamble,' she finished weakly. 'You can't take anything for granted. Not anything. You might work here for weeks and weeks and sell everything you find for a mere song.'

He turned away and stooped to enter the drive. 'You're kidding. You were sure enough earlier on. And I know there are opals here – I feel it in my bones.'

He knew. And Frazer knew otherwise. And she couldn't even begin to explain her own certainty to herself.

For two and a half days she and Rex worked unceasingly. He chiselled and prised and gouged, and Frazer spread the fallen opal dirt and went through it painstakingly, her fingers breaking it up, her eyes alert for any sparkle of fire shown up by the lamp they were using now. She worked more or less automatically, and however hard she battled against it, her mind kept returning to other matters. She thought, in fact, obsessively and incesantly, of Jay Dexter, who didn't come down to the camp or to the diggings, and who must be completely unaware that she and Rex were on to a patch. Fragments of their conversations repeated themselves over and over in her mind. 'Knowledge brings better understanding,' he had said – yet she hadn't confided in him and she hadn't asked him questions that were vital. He had kissed her, called her attractive, asked her to trust him – promised that later he would come to Mingari. And she hadn't trusted him, and she hadn't believed his promises, for the name of Jay Dexter had always been associated in her mind with hatred and treachery and callousness, and her knowledge of him as a real person only confused her.

Now he didn't trust her. If he ever had. Because she had lied to him about Caryl, because she was here alone with Rex – and of course he suspected the worst. Well, if he was still keeping an eye on her, he wouldn't have caught her and Rex out in any tender interludes . . .

She heard herself sigh audibly as she shoved back the pile of dirt she had sifted through and let it fall on top of the pile of mullock on the shaft floor.

It was dirty, tiring, unrewarding work, and though Rex carried on with a fiendish relentlessness, certain that he would be rewarded by at least a handful of precious stones sooner or later, Frazer was lured on by no such hope. Then the patch ran out, and after a moment of disbelief, a groan of disappointment, Rex tossed down the pocket knife and worked again with the pick, and in less than half an hour had, amazingly, struck a new patch.

Quite honestly, Frazer wished he hadn't. It would be so much easier if it was all over – if it was time to pack up and go. There was nothing for her here, she was convinced – and she wasn't thinking only of opals . . .

She straightened from her crouched position and pushed back the hair from her perspiring face, with a dirty hand.

'I've had enough. I'm going to take a bath.'

Rex grunted as he carefully gouged out a small stone with the pocket knife.

'Now? When we're on to a new patch? Don't you want to know what kind of find we've made this time?'

Frazer reached across for the stone he had finally released from the dirt with his fingers, and looked at it carefully. There was not even the glimmer of colour in it, and she was not somehow surprised. 'It won't be any better than the last lot.'

'How do you know?'

'I feel it in my bones,' she said cynically.

The words worried her as she walked slowly back to the camp a few minutes later. The way she had said them – those words that her own father had used so often. What had happened to all her hopes and dreams? – what had happened to her faith?

'Tomorrow – or the next day – I'll go,' she thought, 'I must.' She glanced almost despairingly around. There was not a living creature in sight. Even Rex was hidden below the ground. Jay Dexter, she thought, would be out on the run with his stockmen. Quite possibly she would never see him again. And in a year or two she would have forgotten him completely. Maybe.

She went to the homestead for her bath. When she reached it, it was so quiet it could have been deserted. In the bathroom, she found again the soft towels, the bath salts with their haunting red rose fragrance. It was all a little as though she were acting some part in a fairy tale – though not one with a happy ending, for her at any rate – as she slipped through the empty house and shut herself up in the bathroom. She bathed, washed her hair, rubbed herself dry, and got into clean clothes – rough-dried cotton shirt, her light blue jeans, her sandals. She combed the silver-streaked hair that gave her the look of a stranger, and emerged again.

This time she tiptoed along the hallway and through the house. She opened a door and found an obviously unused bedroom, looked inside another door that stood ajar. Afternoon sunlight made a pattern on the polished floor, and there was a bed with an old-fashioned cover of Indian cotton. A cedar chest with a couple of square, silver-topped boxes, a silver-backed brush that belonged to a man.

She knew it was Jay Dexter's room, and she stood in the doorway almost ready to run, her heart beating fast. There was not a photograph to be seen, not a portrait on the chest. Well, what had she expected, for goodness' sake? A line-up of beautiful half-naked girls? Apart from an open book, face down on the bedside table, the only thing to be seen that you could call personal was a small silver vase that held a couple of dark, velvety red roses. She hadn't noticed it at first – she had thought the scent came from the soap she had used.

As she stood there, a fugitive, an intruder, she felt a strange ache in her heart, and she reflected how much easier it was to hate Jay Dexter than to love him; how much more comfortable. She told herself that she swung uneasily between the two poles, but she refused to admit how easy it would be to go up and over the top and to come down for ever on the side of love. And a hopelessly broken heart.

She tiptoed back down the passage and emerged on the side verandah. And Jay Dexter rose from the cane chair in which he had been sitting.

Frazer's heart plunged and galloped, then everything stood still as he looked at her. Looked and looked.

'I – I came to take a bath,' she said on a breath. She was sure she looked as guilty as if she had been housebreaking, and after all, she had been prowling around where she had no business to be. Her blood curdled at the thought that he might have caught her standing in his bedroom doorway, gaping around.

Her dark eyebrows tilted. 'I realized that. I saw you ride up, as a matter of fact, when I was in the horse paddock.'

'Oh,' said Frazer blankly. She almost gabbled out, 'You're quite wrong about Rex and me.' But there was no possible reason for telling him that – a man like Jay Dexter wouldn't really care one way or the other what Frazer Madigan – Kate, to him – did, furious though he had been with her for lying to him the other day. Hadn't he once even said that who you slept with was a personal matter? The very recollection of that made her colour faintly and avoid his eyes.

Now he commented coolly, 'You've had your head well and truly down the last two or three days, haven't you, Kate?'

'Yes.' She knew she sounded defiant. She noticed he hadn't showered yet. He looked slightly dusty, rather tired, and he wore a checked shirt with the sleeves pushed up and dark, narrow-legged cord trousers. She raised her eyes to his face. 'We've struck a patch, you see.'

She saw his look of quick surprise, followed by a frown. 'A patch? You mean opal?' The dark eyes searched hers, and for a wild moment, just to confound him, she almost said yes. But she had told enough untruths lately, and so she said carefully, moderately, 'So far, it's just been potch and colour. But Rex has just struck a new lot, so?'

'So,' he repeated, and now his eyes were hard. 'You must be feeling on top of the world. You and Rex,' he added deliberately, coupling their names, underlining their association, the fact that they were alone – or that was how it seemed to Frazer.

She put her head up. 'You have the wrong idea about me and Rex – Mr. Dexter. And I don't like it. We're not – I'm not— It's a business partnership, that's all.'

'Yes?' His mouth curved upwards, cynically. 'business partnership that can't accommodate a third person – Rex's girl-friend, you always used to insist. I wonder why not?'

'It's not like that at all,' she stammered, colouring. 'It

was just that — that Caryl wanted a break. She knows there's nothing between me and Rex. She'll — she'll be back any day now.'

'I see,' he said, quite obviously not believing a word she said. 'Am I to take it then that we're to have you around for quite some time to come?'

That, of course, was something he didn't want! He never had. It had been that way from the start — just exactly as it had been when her father came here, she reminded herself bitterly. Well, why should she relieve his mind?

She shrugged and told him carelessly, 'Quite probably.' But she didn't believe it herself. No, she didn't think Frazer Madigan would be staying around at Wandalilli much longer.

He was looking at her unreadably. 'I shall have to come down and take a look at your finds.' He nodded dismissively, then abruptly went into the house.

Turning his back on her. Frazer's heart went cold. So impersonal, so uninterested. She didn't think for a moment that he would even bother to come down and see their finds — that small collection of stones that Rex had brought down from the mine and packed so carefully in a box, cushioning them in the folds of one of his shirts, just as though they were precious opal instead of potch.

But in that she was proved all too soon to be wrong.

Rex was not about when she got back to the camp. She slung her things inside her tent, then began to set the fire. She wondered how long it would be before Rex had worked out this new patch of stone he had traced, and she hoped it wouldn't be long. She didn't want the agony drawn out any longer. It simply didn't even occur to her that he might find any real opal this time. She knew that he never would. Not here. And she wished he would reach the same conclusion — and then they would go. Both of them.

She paused in the act of picking up a likely-looking bit of wood for the fire. Oughtn't someone to wait here for Caryl? Rex wouldn't, so — 'I should,' she thought. And she knew in her heart that she was trying to find some excuse for staying on, when it was quite plainly not good sense to stay. But then it wasn't good sense either to have fallen in love with Jay Dexter, a man whom by all the rules of logic she should hate – and paradoxically did hate, hated all the more *because* she had fallen in love with him.

She had reached this confusing point in her rather sombre reflections when Rex appeared. He had been down to the river, his hair was wet, he had got into clean shorts and shirt, and he was swinging a towel.

'Hi, Fraze, you all clean and pretty again too? That's a really sexy perfume you're wearing. Did it have the desired effect on your boy friend up at the homestead?'

He had come close, and she felt her hand itching to slap his face, but she controlled herself. Soon she would never have to see Rex Byfield again, so she merely snapped a handful of twigs and said flatly, 'If I were a man I'd probably punch your nose in for using that tone.'

'I'm sure you would,' he agreed with a grin. 'You did even better than that the other night, didn't you? Still you're quite decidedly a female, Fraze, and right at this moment you're very nice to be near.'

Frazer gave him a look of contempt and turned her back on him, and in a second he had locked his arms hard about her from behind and was kissing the back of her neck, and for a moment she was completely helpless.

She had only begun to struggle when he released her, because they both heard someone approaching on horseback.

Frazer looked up, colour surging into her face, then receding to leave it pale. Jay Dexter had ridden down to take a look at their find.

His eyes, black and glinting and narrow, met hers and she knew as plainly as if he had said it aloud that he was remembering what she had said less than an hour ago. 'Caryl knows there's nothing between me and Rex.'

'You're busy,' he said, his voice the cold steel of a dagger so that Frazer felt herself shiver as if she had been physically hurt. 'I must apologize for coming at the wrong time.' And then, without even a glance at Rex, he turned his horse's head and rode away.

Rex said, 'What the hell did he want?'

'Oh, what do you think? To see our *find*,' Frazer snapped, though tears of mortification and something else were stinging at the back of her eyes. 'And you had to be—' She stopped in fury, then burst out, 'If you ever touch me again, I'll – I'll kill you!'

Rex stared at her. 'Don't tell me you've fallen for the cattleman,' he jeered. 'I've told you before – girls like you aren't everyone's cup of tea. You should learn to be a bit realistic, Frazer. And that brings me to my own bit of realism – that new patch I found is a complete wash-out. Five or six bits of dead-looking potch and it's cut out. I've had this dump. So forget about your heart for a little while, and think about what we're going to do now, Frazer Madigan.'

'What *we're* going to do?' Frazer had fought back her tears, and she ignored his gibes. She was glad the patch had cut out, and she couldn't see the last of Rex soon enough. 'You can do whatever you like,' she told him. 'Don't bother consulting me.'

'I might make for Lightning Ridge,' he said after a moment, completely ignoring her obvious hostility. 'Why don't you come along too?'

'With you? You must be joking.'

'I'm serious. You're a great girl to have around. So what about it?'

'No. And what I do is my own business. I just don't want to discuss anything with you. Not anything.'

After that, communication between them practically ceased. Frazer fixed the fire and prepared a meal and they ate it in silence. When they had finished she cleared up and went into her tent, leaving Rex sitting alone by the embers of the fire.

That night was one of the most sleepless she had ever known. Her whole life seemed to have gone awry. She had been just as blind and illogical as Caryl in falling in love, and as well – and perhaps even worse – she had somewhere along the way lost her faith in her father. She knew that she wouldn't use Caryl as an excuse to stay on here. She would go tomorrow.

At the first crack of daylight she was up. She got into jeans and boots and jacket and went up to the mine. And she knew as she stood there on the rough slope, in the light that was still grey and cheerless, that she had come for another reason as well as that of making a last sad pilgrimage to the place where her father had worked. She wanted to see the stockmen – and Jay Dexter – riding out from Wandalilli homestead.

But she didn't see them, and she didn't realize until much later it was because it was Sunday.

Standing shivering in the cool dawn breeze, she faced the facts of her own disillusionment. She had come here a silly wide-eyed girl, following a dream, seeing all life through the eyes of a child, and she had come up against inescapable reality. The man she had hated in theory for so long – Jay Dexter – had taught her in the hardest way possible how to be a woman. She had fallen in love with him and he, so much older and more experienced, had amused himself with her for a while and now cynically accepted that she and Rex were lovers.

Most disillusioning of all, as she looked down into the vacant shadows of the shaft, she knew she had lost her belief in her father. There was nothing here. He had been wrong, wrong, wrong. *She* had been right when she had been so positive Rex would find nothing. He should have been satisfied with those two gemstones he had found long ago and given to her, she thought wearily. They were surely the best any rational man could ever hope to find. And when he had talked as he had – about lifting his shining flame from its cradle in the dark earth, saying all those colourful romantic things that had so taken hold of her imagination – shouldn't she have realized before this that it was all no more than the phantom hope that led the opal miner on and on forever? How many, many times in her childhood she had heard him say that *this* time he knew. And at an emotional fourteen or fifteen, when she had lost him so suddenly, she had been all too ready to believe that *this* time it had been only death that had kept him from attaining his ideal. She saw it differently now. Her father had been a hopeless dreamer. She could even accept now that it had been fate, not Jay Dexter, that had brought his life to a close. The Old Man – Jay's father – had died in an accident. 'Death is inevitable,' Jay had told her realistically. 'And often unacceptable.'

'Poor Dad,' she thought now, staring sightlessly down into the mine, where his last fantastic hopes now lay dead. With a sort of pity she saw him no longer as the father in whose footsteps she had followed so devotedly, so determinedly. She saw him as the man he must have been. A man so obsessed by his dream that it twisted and coloured his whole outlook on life, blinding him to reason and reality. He had been like a man gambling, unable to leave it alone. It was a salutary experience to see your father, your childhood, your very self through new eyes. Deep inside, Frazer wanted to cry and cry for all that was lost. To cry like a child . . .

When she went back to the camp Rex was up. He had lit the fire, and begun dismantling his tent and packing up.

'What'd you find, Frazer?' he sneered. 'Did you get a guide line from the spirit world where to look next? A pointer from the fool who dug that mine in the first place?'

'Don't talk like that about—' Frazer flared angrily, then bit back the words.

Rex was looking at her hard, half amused. 'About who?'

'About – anything. Just – keep quiet.' Frazer went into her tent, unaware for once of the beauty brought by the sun as it came up over the edge of the world, flooding the plain with vermilion and gold. She wished Rex would vanish – disappear. She wished that she could go to sleep for a hundred years and wake up not remembering a thing. She wished that somehow, miraculously, every-thing would come right. That there was opal in the mine for her father, that Jay Dexter – that Jay Dexter loved her.

And that last was the most futile stupid wish of all. She felt even angrier with herself than she had been with Rex.

With shaking hands she began to pack her things. Her poverty pot with the stones still in it – she unwrapped them and looked at them for a moment, her violet eyes sad. In time those would comfort her more, she would tell herself that this was a little piece of her father's dream come true, material proof of the fact that he hadn't been entirely deluded—

When she went outside again, Rex had breakfasted and for the time being he was not in sight. He had packed up Caryl's tent as well as his own, she noted, and the place was beginning to look half deserted. She wasn't hungry, but she built up the fire to make herself some tea. As she filled the billy from the water-bottle, she noticed that the box in which they had kept the stones from the shaft was empty. Rex must have packed the potch away in his swag, and Frazer felt a sudden deep contempt for him – to be so mean as not even to offer to share those pieces of potch and colour! No doubt he didn't trust her, and was going to find out from someone else whether what she had told him was true or not. Well, it was. And he was welcome to the lot. It was the meanness and smallness of his attitude that she so despised. And to think that Caryl had imagined herself in love with such a man!

She had finished packing up and so had Rex, and they had exchanged scarcely a word when Frazer heard the sound of a motor – and coming bumping along by the river was a taxi! Frazer stared, unbelieving. It pulled up some distance from the camp, the door opened and a girl with bright red hair emerged.

Caryl! Frazer felt her heart lift. In seconds they were greeting each other.

'Caryl – oh, how marvellous to see you! I was hoping

you'd come—'

Caryl was staring at the place where the tents had been. 'You're leaving!' She looked from Frazer to Rex, and as he turned to face her, her green eyes widened. She had never seen him shaved before, and it obviously knocked her off balance.

Rex said casually, 'Hi, Caryl. You've come in the nick of time. We're moving off any minute now. We've got all your gear packed up ready for you. I was wondering what we'd do with it.'

Caryl looked at him with a curious expression on her face, as if he were almost a complete stranger. She said not quite steadily, 'I – I hardly knew you. And Frazer – you stayed? I didn't think you would.'

'Oh sure, Frazer stayed,' Rex assured her. 'She can look after herself.'

Caryl looked from one to the other of them. 'What's – what's been happening while I've been away?'

'Plenty,' said Rex, before Frazer could even begin to reply. 'Have you got time to hear? You've got a taxi waiting.'

Caryl shrugged. 'It doesn't matter. It can wait.'

'You mean,' said Rex, smiling crookedly, 'you weren't planning to join them again?'

Caryl coloured, but she said firmly, 'No. I don't really like the outback. I'm a city girl, I guess. I went to White Cliffs – it was hideous and I didn't find a thing.' She looked at Frazer almost apologetically.

'You'd have done better staying here,' Rex said. 'We struck a seam. Didn't we, Frazer? – just like you always promised.'

'Really?' exclaimed Caryl. 'How fabulous!'

Rex's eyebrows went up. 'Now don't get too excited. We found a seam, I said – but no opals. Only a lot of rubbish. So don't change your mind all of a sudden about joining us – it's not worth it.'

'I wasn't going to change my mind,' said Caryl. 'I'm collecting my things and going home.'

Rex looked at her and pursed his lips. 'I'll stick to the

motorbike, if you don't mind. I'm going to Lightning Ridge.'

Caryl's lips twisted ironically. 'The bike's yours. I told you that all along. I don't want it back.'

'Very generous,' he said, not at all grateful. 'Seeing you got nothing out of it. Anyhow, I'll make you a promise, Caryl. I'll deliver it back to you – personally – if I strike a bit of luck at the Ridge.'

'Don't bother,' said Caryl, her colour high. She looked at Frazer who had been listening in silence, and had reached the conclusion that at least with the rational part of her mind Caryl was through with Rex. As for whether she still had any feeling for him deep inside, who could know that, except Caryl herself? 'Are you going to Lightning Ridge too, Frazer?'

Frazer said, 'No,' and Rex cut in, 'Not she! Fraze and I have finished playing games together – but believe me, we've certainly had some fun! She threw a boot at my head one night – didn't you, Fraze? She wasn't brought up nicely like you, Caryl – I reckon before she landed at that boarding school for young ladies she'd done a stint on the opal fields.' He looked at Frazer, mocking, eyes narrowed.

Frazer felt the blood go from her face. She felt a little dizzy. She didn't want Rex guessing things about her past. She had made certain admissions to Jay, but to Rex – never. He was looking at her pallor, watching her reaction with a cruel half smile, and suddenly he slapped his thigh. 'That's it! *That's it!* It was Frazer's old man who dug the mine up there. Of course it was! It explains poor old Fraze in full. Her father was a screwball – a nut. No wonder your uncle had to take you in charge, Fraze! What happened? Did your old man die in the sun out here? Did he go off his head looking for opals in a place where they don't exist? Are his bones bleaching out on the plains? Poor old Frazer – coming out here to follow a kid's dream, and find the treasure he missed out on! It would be really funny if I hadn't been such a sucker and believed you knew something – and worked my guts out for damn all.'

For seconds, while he ranted, Frazer stood frozen. And then – and then she wanted to kill him. She had thought she knew something about hatred, now she realized that until this minute she never had. Rex – *Rex* mocking her father!

She broke in on Caryl's heated angry exclamation, 'What a rotten way to talk—'

'Be quiet, Caryl.' Her head was up, her cheeks were flaming. 'Yes, my father dug that mine, and he knew what he was doing. Just never mind why he didn't carry on here – he found opals, fabulous opals, in other places that would make your eyes fall out with envy. You're – you're not fit to breathe his name. There's – there's not an opal in the world that would shine for you – it's no wonder you didn't find anything—'

Suddenly she couldn't go on. She turned her back abruptly and half blind with tears, began to move in the direction of her tent. But her tent wasn't there any more! She realized it with a sharp shock. She had packed up – given in. She had been about to walk out on her father. She – Frazer Madigan. Refusing to believe! For a second she hated herself almost as much as she hated Rex . . . Of course she wasn't going. If her father had come here, it was because he *knew*—

With a sudden determination, and with hands that were rock-steady, she began to unpack her tent, and she looked up when Caryl came and said timidly, 'Don't be upset, Frazer. I'm sorry about what Rex said – he's hateful, cruel, I can't think why I was ever so mad about him. I'm – I'm sorry about your father, but don't stay here – please! Come in the taxi with me. We'll stay the night in Minning and then – then I'll come home with you to Mingari. I'll—'

Frazer shook her head. Her eyes were dry, her mind clear. 'I'm not upset, Caryl. It's sweet of you to try to help, but I've got to stay here, that's all. It's what I want to do – it's what I came for. I know you won't believe it, but – it was because of Rex we didn't find anything. I feel it in my bones.' She repeated the words slowly, 'I feel it in my bones.'

Caryl didn't try to persuade her any more. Frazer ignored Rex completely. She fixed up her tent and put her things inside, and then she began to walk to the taxi with Caryl to see her off. Caryl said, 'I picked a dud, didn't I? I really messed you up, bringing Rex here. I don't suppose I was really in love with him. It was just that he was — different, exciting. It's funny, but without his beard he looks so kind of ordinary. I guess I've just got over him. And I *hate* him for talking to you like he did. About your father,' she finished awkwardly.

Frazer managed a smile. 'I should have told you about all that long ago. I will some time. I didn't want to tell Rex — and at school — well, everyone would have thought it odd.'

'Come down to Sydney before May,' Caryl invited after a moment. 'Come and stay awhile before we go to Europe. I wish you'd come now — I don't like you staying here on your own.'

Alone? Frazer thought fleetingly of Jay Dexter. But she wasn't staying because of him. She had been as deluded as Caryl in thinking she was in love with him. She couldn't be — for reasons that had existed for several years. She told Caryl, 'I have to stay. But I'll be all right. And I can always go if I want to.'

Behind her, she heard Rex start up his motorbike, and as they reached the taxi he went skidding by, calling derisively, 'Write me a letter when you find the treasure trove, Fraze!'

Caryl's taxi had gone and Frazer had walked back almost as far as her tent when she saw something shining on the ground, half hidden in a clump of rough spiky grass. Her heart stood still. She stopped to pick it up.

Her poverty pot! The lid was gone, and it was empty.

CHAPTER TEN

Rex.

He had taken it when she was walking to the taxi with Caryl. She knew with a dreadful fatalism that it had happened like that. But how had he found it? How had he known? Her mind leaped back to that night she had come back to the camp and imagined he had been in her tent. He must have found out then – he must have planned even then to steal those two stones before they parted company. She felt full of an agonized rage. Her father's most precious finds – and Rex had stolen them. Oh, he was a dingo!

Her mind worked feverishly, but she knew it was no use riding after him. She would never catch up with him, and even if she did, what could she do? It was one thing to fetch him a whack on the jaw with her boot when he came to her tent, but this was another matter altogether. If she could only call on someone for help. Jay Dexter— But she cut off that line of thought almost before it had begun.

At that moment it seemed to Frazer that her happiness in life had reached its very lowest ebb, and for an instant, even her idea of staying on to vindicate her father seemed futile. All the same, she made herself a sandwich, and in twenty minutes flat she was marching up to the slope in her working gear.

She carried on where Rex had left off. At least he hadn't taken the pick or the shovel, and she crouched in the drive, the lamp lit, examining the walls and roof for any telltale redness or grittiness in the opal dirt that could indicate the presence of the seam. For hours she stayed there under the ground, chipping away in defence of her father. And somewhere along the line, for no particular reason, she changed direction. 'Opal and I – we warm to each other.' The words came into her mind of their own accord. She was widening the drive now instead of lengthening it, working mechanically, mindless, yet intent . . .

Behind her in the shaft there was an unearthly red glow as the sun went down and the sky took fire. And then – just then – Frazer heard it. The chink as of glass as the pick struck something hard in the opal dirt. A sound clear and sharp as a musical note. She couldn't believe it. It couldn't be true. Her heart stopped, her faith rushed back in a flood, warm and emotional, and suddenly it was as if her father was there beside her. 'I told you we'd find it, Frazer – I told you it was here – my Wandalilli Princess.' So clear was his voice, so warm and real his presence . . .

Now her pulses began to race. She saw the live and vibrant flash of orange and vermilion winking at her from the tunnel wall, and her heart lifted as though the heavens were opening. It was like light shining down – like rainbow light – and she knew – she knew with tears in her eyes that her father had been right. And when she tossed down the pick and prised gently, gently, with her fingers, and lifted out the small hard stone – rubbed away the dirt from around it, caught its fiery gleam – then she knew that here was the stone her father had been seeking all his life. There would be others in the patch, but this – this was his Wandalilli Princess, the beautiful shining opal for which he had searched with all the ardour of a knight in quest of the Grail. She held it in her hand and she knew. For him, it would have been the answer to his heart's desire. For Frazer – because of him, because it vindicated him, proved him no mere crank – because of these things she cherished it, and the tears ran down her cheeks.

But the tears were for something else as well, for her own lost dream. *She* could never attain what her heart desired, the love of one man who, whatever he had done in the past, was the one man her soul cried out for in hunger. She thought she would forgive him everything – if only she had the chance.

She had wrapped the stone carefully in a tissue and put it in the pocket of her jeans when a shadow fell across the shaft. She looked up and saw through eyes that were still full of tears the dark figure of a man against the evening sky. Because of the fragile joy in her heart, she thought it was Jay Dexter and she wanted to cry out to him, 'See what I've found!' And she wanted him to put his arms around her and to kiss her and kiss her . . .

She dashed away her tears as she swivelled round from her crouched position to move out of the tunnel. And then she saw that it was not Jay. It was Rex. In the second she realized it, he jumped, and as her feet reached the mullock-strewn floor of the shaft, he was there too. He moved close until he was almost on top of her and he said menacingly, 'Well, Frazer, what are you doing down here the minute my back's turned? There were things you didn't tell me about this shaft, weren't there? What have you found? Come on now – hand it over.'

With a sudden movement he grabbed hold of her wrist and twisted her arm up behind her back so that she gasped with pain and the tears flew to her eyes. 'You're not going to get away with anything, Frazer Madigan.'

Frazer never knew what would have happened next, because someone else sprang into the shaft, and it was Jay Dexter. In a flash Frazer was free, and everything was confusion in the small confined space. Jay had punched Rex on the jaw and now the two men were wrestling together on the loose mullock of the shaft floor. Frazer's heart hammered as she listened to the thuds, the grunts, the heavy breathing, the occasional muffled exclamation. She knew she had better keep out of the way! Using the toe-holds in the shaft wall – things that she and Rex had never bothered about, but that her father had cut and that she knew were there – she scrambled up and out of the shaft until she was able to crouch on the ground at the top and watch.

She didn't cry out 'Stop!' like many girls would have – like Caryl would have. She didn't cover her eyes or even feel fear as the two men fought. In her mind there was not the slightest doubt as to who would be the victor, and a small voice at the back of her mind reminded her, 'He was watching – he was keeping an eye on me.' She was aware of a feeling of wild excitement.

At last Rex slumped gasping against the wall. Jay, breathing hard, climbed out of the shaft and stood there for a few seconds. Then he called down, 'Come on, Byfield – get yourself up here and we'll carry on in the open, if that's what you want.'

Frazer had straightened up, and she stood not twelve inches from Jay as Rex hauled himself out. Blood ran from his nose and from a gash in his lip, and his breathing was hoarse and painful. He said, his voice a croak, 'I've had enough – I'm beaten!'

He turned and would have moved away, but Frazer shot out, 'You stole my father's opals. I want them back.'

She saw his eyes, ugly and cold as pebbles, flick across shiftily to Jay, and she saw Jay's hands move just slightly. Then Rex reached into his pocket and took something from it. He flung it on the ground with an oath and went stumbling down the slope. Frazer's heart began to thud and her limbs felt weak as she moved to pick up the scrap of silk that had once been part of her father's scarf. Her fingers trembled as she untied the knot and the two stones slipped out into her hand. She looked at them for a moment before she wrapped them up again and put them in her pocket. Dimly, she was aware of the sound of a motorbike starting up and she knew that Rex was going. She raised her eyes to Jay who had stood silently, watching her. A few large pallid stars hung in the colourless sky and his eyes looked black in the rich dark tan of his face. There was a small cut at the side of his mouth and she could see the black line of blood already dried.

Suddenly she knew she wanted to have his arms around her – to touch his mouth with her fingers— She said huskily, 'Thank you for coming to my rescue – Mr. Dexter. And for being there to back me up when I asked Rex for my opals.'

She saw his eyebrows tilt and the long line of his mouth alter slightly, and she felt his hard look.

'No trouble,' he said. 'I'll admit it gave me some satisfaction to—' He stopped and started again. 'I just hoped I wouldn't be breaking up anything when I came over to investigate. I saw your two friends making their departure earlier on, tents and all – as it's Sunday, I happened to be around all day. I'd observed that *you'd* gone back to the mine, Kate' – his voice was faintly ironic – 'whether to dig or to weep I didn't know. I didn't want to intrude, but I didn't want to take chances either.' He paused. 'I take it the *partnership's* broken up.'

They had begun to move down the slope towards the camp and the lone tent, and Frazer hated the way he had stressed that one word. And if he thought she might have been weeping over Rex— She felt a little thread of despair draw through her heart. She didn't really think he would be interested in her love or her forgiveness ... She told him briefly, 'Yes, it's broken up. And it was what I always told you – a business partnership.'

They walked on. 'I can't think you quarrelled over your finds,' he suggested.

'No,' she agreed quickly. 'We – Rex – found only potch. So he decided to give it away and try his luck at Lightning Ridge. Or somewhere,' she added vaguely, to underline the fact that she didn't care in the slightest.

'So you didn't want to go with him. What kept you here?'

'I knew there were opals here,' said Frazer after a moment. She sent him a half defiant look from her violet-blue eyes. They were walking a foot apart from each other, and there was something electric in the air.

They had reached the camp now, and she could see his station wagon beyond the trees. The light had faded and his dark face didn't look so dark, but his eyes were black and shadowy, and she knew they were searching her face. He said, 'So you've been working down under the ground all day, have you?'

Frazer said 'Yes.' And as she said it, she had a very

clear mental image of herself – Frazer Madigan, filthy – yes, she was really filthy from her hours under the ground – hands, hair, face, clothes, boots – the lot. What a picture she must make! What must he be thinking now as he looked at her the way he was doing? What Rex had said was only too true. A girl like Frazer Madigan was not to every man's taste. Far from it.

She heard him make some soft exclamation beneath his breath, then his hands reached out and they were on her arms in a grip that was so hard it was cruel. She had no idea what was going to happen next, but she heard herself breathe out – as if she *had* to – 'I – hate you, Jay Dexter.' For an instant he held her motionless, and then he pulled her almost savagely against him.

'That's a lie, Kate,' he murmured, then his lips were on hers and he kissed her and kissed her until she had no resistance left, and he could have done what he liked with her.

They were both completely breathless when he relaxed his hold on her and looked down into her face.

'Well, do you still say you hate me – *Frazer Madigan*?'

Frazer Madigan! She gasped as if she had been slapped in the face. She stammered out, 'If you know *that* – you *know* that I hate you.'

'I'm afraid I don't,' he said. 'In fact, I know you damn well don't hate me. Quite the contrary, if you were only adult enough to admit it ... I do know, though, that you've got some hang-up about your father, so let's have it all out, shall we? I've waited long enough for you to be ready to talk.'

She stared at him. 'Long enough? What do you mean? You only found out just now – when Rex called me that—'

'Oh no.' He shook his head and his eyes were mercilessly searching. 'I worked it out long ago – the night you told me your father had been a miner, and that you'd spent years of your life on the opal fields. Remember? I didn't know the reason for your secrecy and I didn't push you. I admit I tried to make it easy for you to talk – to give you openings – but you wouldn't play. If you had – if I *had* pushed you – maybe you'd never have been in danger of being knocked out or even throttled down there in the mine this evening. You'd have been safe up at the homestead with me.'

Frazer gasped, 'I wouldn't! I know what you think about my morals, but – but it's not true. I'm not – I'd never – I *wouldn*'t be up there with you—'

She heard his impatient exclamation— 'Oh, for God's sake!' – then he had taken her hard by the shoulders. 'All right, I've jumped ahead a bit – I didn't mean I was going to seduce you. Not when I had it in mind to ask you to marry me. And that,' he finished ironically, 'is one very good reason why we've got to get all this thrashed out. Now.'

Marry him! Frazer's head was spinning. 'I'd never marry you, Jay Dexter! Never! Because of what you did to my father.'

His eyes bored into her. 'What did I do to your father, Kate? Come on, out with it – let's have it. Let's hear what lunatic ideas are shut up in that brain of yours.'

'You – you wouldn't take him to the doctor when he was so sick,' she quavered. And as she said it, she knew it couldn't possibly be true – that she had never really been able to believe it since first she met him. She floundered on, 'Not till it was too late – not for two days. I know – you can't fool me – my father wrote me a letter the day he felt the pains—'

'Good God! Is that the opinion you have of me? Your father and I were beginning to understand each other . . . Now listen to me, Kate. I take it this is the story you were talking about when you first hit Wandalilli. And you fouled things up yourself by telling me you were Cathleen Dwight – and a newspaper reporter!' Suddenly he stopped, and when he spoke again it was more gently. 'I'm sorry to be so hard on you at a time like this, Kate – Frazer. But you deserve it. Your father's death is something you just have to come to terms with, and no one was to blame for it. Do you want me to tell you the story here and now, or will you come up to the homestead and get yourself cleaned up first?'

She looked around her almost dazedly at a landscape that was all but dark, at yellow lights that shone from the homestead in its sheltering trees.

'Here,' she said. 'Now.' Where my tent and my motorbike are close, she thought.

She heard him sigh. 'Very well. It's the story of two tragedies, Kate . . . I didn't know your father well. He was prickly, like you. And I think he had a down on station owners. But we'd begun to get on together – after I'd stitched up a cut in his foot.' He paused, and Frazer didn't trust herself to speak to explain, to question. She stood close to Jay, listening – nervy, tensed up, digging at the ground with the toe of one dirty boot. 'There was a muster on, otherwise he wouldn't have been here on his own. The men were camped thirty odd miles away, and Dolly had gone to visit some of her relatives across the Darling. Ordinarily, the Old Man and I'd have been back to the homestead to sleep, but on the first day he had an accident and had to be taken to hospital. I told you about that. Remember?'

She looked up and nodded. Yes, of course she remembered. Listening, she began dimly to understand how it had all happened – to feel a gradual release of the tension that had built up inside of her. She didn't dig round in the dirt with her boot any more. She stood straight, head up, one hand on her breast, the other in her pocket, quiet, thoughtful.

'I was away four days at the hospital while my father was dying,' Jay said. 'I didn't know a thing about your father's tragedy till Joe – one of my stockmen – told me on that last day.'

'What – happened?' breathed Frazer. She didn't resist when Jay took her hand and drew her against him.

'Joe found him in his tent – a very sick man – when he drove in to the homestead for more supplies for the muster camp. He took him straight to the hospital, but it was too late.'

Frazer closed her eyes. She felt the warmth of tears between her lids. She felt pain for her father, but it was a remote pain, because what had happened was over now. All the bitterness was gone, somehow, and Jay— She felt his arms around her, drawing her close, and she whispered, 'I thought – I thought you wouldn't help him. Oh, I'm sorry – I'm sorry – I should have known you could never have been like that! At least – *he* knew—'

Jay kissed her again, gently, and she dried her tears, and he told her, 'Well, we'll talk about it more later, Kate. Meanwhile, I'm not going to let you sleep in your solitary little tent tonight. Dolly's at the homestead, and you'll sleep there. Besides' – drawing a finger down her cheek, his white teeth showing in a smile – 'you badly need a bath. You are quite incredibly dirty, my Kate.'

Her violet-blue eyes were wide, questioning. 'But you kissed me, Jay—'

'I'd kiss you if you were caked in mud,' he said. And added so simply that she was close to tears again, 'I love you, Kate.'

She looked down at herself and spread her hands. 'Me? Frazer Madigan?' she said wonderingly.

His wide mouth curled up at one corner and he pulled her to him again.

'You, Frazer Madigan,' he said, and strangely, the name sounded wonderful as he said it. 'Boots – dirt – prickliness and all.' And he set his lips against hers to prove it . . .

Later, she thought – much later – would be soon enough to tell him about the Wandalilli Princess. But now – and from now on – all her passion was for him.

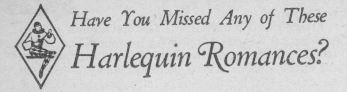

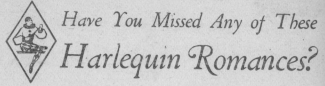

Have You Missed Any of These Harlequin Romances?

All books listed 75c

Have you missed any of these . . .

Have you missed any of these . . .

Harlequin Presents..

All books listed 95c